Mirror Me this

A NOVEL BY
B.T. JULIAN

TATE PUBLISHING, LLC

WALTON CROSSING

DEDICATION

HEY! My name's B.T. Julian and you have
just picked up my first book. I am 13 years old
and I love to write. ^-^ This book is dedicated
to my mother, Nancy, my father, Mike, my
surrogate parents Maureen and John, and
my two best friends in the entire world who
are like my sisters: Jordan and Victoria!
Thank you for supporting me
through everything, guys!
B.T.

TABLE OF CONTENTS

PREFACE

May 18, 2005

This book is a pure figment of my imagination. I was just thinking one day and a lot of the time when I write books I get the entire story mapped out in my head before I write it on the computer. I come from a modest family that consists of mostly just my father and me. My dad supports me in everything I do and I thank him for that, but that's what the "dedication" is for. Really this book wouldn't have come about if it hadn't been for my love of books. At the age of six I could be found in the library at school, gobbling up as many books as I could get my hands on. I always felt that the more I read, the smarter I became. As I like to say, books are the best tools we have. I actually began to write at the age of seven. I started by writing short stories, or starting a chapter and then stopping because my mind couldn't fully grasp a whole story. I go back now and read through the notebooks upon notebooks that I wrote in and laugh. I would start something and then stop and then start again. I guess that's what I've always done. I've written books and things of the sort but this is my first book ever! It came about last Christmas . . . I believe it was about December 20, 2004 when I started this book. I finished it on the 25th as I often do. Many people have been telling me to send my books in so that's what I did, I took a chance and without my father's permission sent it in to Tate—which brings us to the present point. I thank all the people at Tate Publishing for being so helpful and supportive, even when I was being a brat about editing.

Love,
B.T. Julian

The Message

"Help me."

Rick read the message again on his screen; it was scaring him. His heart was racing as he replied to the unknown sender.

"With what?" he asked the sender and waited for a reply. He leaned back in his chair crossing his strong arms across his chest. Freaky things like this always happened to him. Ever since he was a little kid he had been seeing things and solving problems for things beyond this realm. He wasn't a witch; he wasn't a psychic he wasn't a mutant, he was just a teenage kid with a knack for attracting trouble. He was 16 and his parents home-schooled him. He brushed his long spiky brown hair out of his face. His blue eyes searched the screen as the reply came.

"I'm lost," came the reply.

"Where are you?" Rick asked and the person logged off. He couldn't figure it out but he did know that something freaky was going on.

"Well, what was it?" Rick turned around and almost jumped out of his skin, behind him was his friend, he had died hundreds of years ago but he had come back and Rick had saved him from almost certain . . . errr, well, death . . . something like that. He was a tall young man with piercing red eyes. He was wearing a blue English Army uniform. His hair was short and black and pulled back behind his head in a small pony tail.

"Jeez, Marshall you scared me," Rick said to the ghost.

"Well, ghosts do that you know," the phantom replied. Rick nodded and stood up.

"I don't know who it was . . . but . . . whoever it was needs help . . . whatever that means," Rick said. He pulled on his shirt to go for a walk.

"Care if I come?" The apparition asked him.

Rick shook his head and walked out into the hot Hawaiian sun.

"Well, Rick where are we going today?" Marshall asked excitedly, he loved to go with Rick because he was excited by new things and was amused by the simplest things. Such as . . . "Rick look here. . . ." The phantom pulled an antenna out of a car.

"Marshall, stop! People are strange when they see things like that," Rick scolded the specter.

"Well, aren't we the cranky Sue today?" the ghost replied.

"Shut-up, will you please?" Rick asked him.

"Well I never, I'll leave." The English man huffed and floated off.

Rick lived in a town that most people never knew existed. It was a small town and it was filled with all sorts of people. They had a few Areos—or the 'angelic' race—the girls were perfect and some Areos had wings. Rick was an Areos but he wasn't born with wings. There were a bunch of gremlins that lived behind the diner and other people lived there—an odd assortment of races. There were a few tall elves and a small amount of Dryads. Rick sighed as he walked up the sand dunes and sat down under the tree he loved the most.

"Hey! Rick, I thought you would be up here." An Areos female came running forward. She was beautiful. Her eyes were catlike with catlike pupils and yellow grayish eyes. Her tanned body was perfectly shaped and smooth. Her hair was long, cascading down past her waist; a light brown color with blonde high lights and the last three inches of it were almost like bed springs. Her bikini was white.

"Hey, Lexa what's up?" he asked. Her mother had died when she was a young girl so she was being raised by her father who was also an Areos.

"Nothing, how's my ghoul?" she asked him. That's what she called her best friend. Another Areo sran forward who was just as beautiful. Her hair was short and chocolate brown The vivacious angel always had it up in some kind of strange fashion. Today it was up in two loose buns on the back of her head. Her eyes were brilliant green and, just like her best friend, she had a perfectly shaped body.

"Great, how are you two?" Rick asked. Kari was the other's name and she was Lexa's best friend; the three of them were all friends.

"I'm tired, I've been out there swimming for *hours*," Kari laughed.

"Where have *you* been all morning?" Lexa asked Rick and he sighed.

"I got this message earlier from some unknown sender. It's creeping me out."

"Well, maybe we should check it out. What'd they say?" Lexa asked. Lexa was the party girl, Rick was their resident ghoul and Kari was the brains of the operation.

"'Help me,'" Rick said simply. Both girls leaned in curiously.

"Looks like we've got an all nighter, eh?" Kari said to him and he nodded.

"I don't know . . . it was so weird, they said they were lost . . . and I asked where they were and they signed off," Rick said to the girls.

"Well then, how about your house, your room, DVDs popcorn and a spook?" Lexa smiled.

"Sure, but I don't think Marshall will want to come out, I ticked him off this morning," Rick told them.

"Sure, he will—he can never resist a party." Kari laughed.

"You guys are the best friends." Rick laughed as they hugged him.

A ways away another boy watched them then suddenly jumped out, squirting them with a water gun, the girls shrieked and Rick laughed, warding off the spray.

"RYU!" the soaked Areos cried at the young man who was laughing hysterically.

"Ra, you two should have seen your faces!" Ryu laughed. He was tall, the same age as Rick and another one of their best friends. He had come over from Australia but he was born in Egypt.

"Ryu, that was great." Rick laughed. Ryu was tanned and muscular, and he was half Areos and half human.

"I know—wasn't it?" Ryu laughed and both girls tackled him, slamming him into the ground. Rick smiled mischievously and picked up the water gun.

"Step away from the Areos or I will have to squirt you till you freeze," Rick told them. They both stood up and walked away.

"AGH! . . . that hurt," Ryu laughed. Rick smiled and threw the gun back to him.

"Save that for later—we might need it," Rick told him and Ryu nodded.

"I understand, Captain," Ryu said, saluting Rick.

THE UNKNOWN

Promptly at 7 o'clock p.m. Rick heard his door bell ring and he ran up the stairs. He walked towards the door wearing jeans but, he had his shirt in his hand; his perfectly carved body a bronze color.

"Hello ladies." He bowed mockingly as they walked in.

"Hello Rick," the girls replied and walked in.

"You two twins or what?" he asked. Lexa was wearing a pair of loose blue jeans that were folded up at the bottom to her calves. Her shirt was a white tank top. She walked into the kitchen, her hair up in a braid.

"Not even close Rick," Kari replied. Her hair was up Japanese style, her sleek hair was pulled up again in two buns, but protruding from the buns two chopsticks could be seen from each. She was wearing a pair of jean shorts and had on a shirt that was too big for her, and the back of the shirt was tucked in the back of her shorts. Rick's pet sand fox hopped down the stairs and pounced on Kari's head.

"Hello, Danny." Kari petted the fox.

"Good evening, Mr. and Mrs. Daniels. How are you?" Kari asked.

"Well now—how are you girls tonight?" Mr. Daniels asked looking up from his paper.

"We're great. Schools about to start . . . Rick you're coming this year right?" Lexa replied looking up at Rick as he nodded.

"Cool, you're coming to school?" Kari asked him and he nodded again.

"I can't wait, I've never been to a real school before." Rick smiled at his parents.

"I know! This is so exciting," his mother said and Rick ushered the girls down the stairs before his parents said anything. The downstairs was all one room. It was decorated with pictures of movie stars and bands; pictures of his friends and family were pasted across the walls in a profusion of images and memories. His bed was pushed into one corner, was unmade and covered in clothes. His laptop was sitting next to his desktop. His laptop was older than his desktop but he liked it better. His stereo was on his dresser that was against another wall. His floor wasn't carpeted; just hardwood. In one corner next to his computers was a big screen TV, DVD player, X-Box, Nintendo Game Cube, and PlayStation 2. To top it all off, Marshall was sitting in the middle of the floor, spinning around in a circle trying to watch the baby fox chase its tail.

"This thing runs fast," the Englishman said stiffly as he stopped spinning to face them.

"It's a fox, maybe we should start calling you 'Curious George,'" Rick told the ghoul as they sat down on the futon couch. The girls would normally end up sitting on his bed and he would end up on the futon . . . how, he never knew. Then as Lexa kneeled down to choose a movie there was a 'ding' , and they all turned around as a message came up on the computer screen.

"Help me . . . please help . . . ."

"What do you need?" Rick asked and the girls watched over his shoulder as the reply came.

"I need help," the note said.

"Okay where are you?" Rick asked.

"I don't know . . . I don't know . . ." the sender replied.

"Describe it," he said and they watched in anticipation. Another note came.

"I'm in a dark place, it's strange," the sender replied.

"Why are you sending me this message?"

"Because . . ." The note stopped there as the person signed off.

"Maybe their connection is bad?" Kari said.

"Well, if they want to talk to you that bad, they'll get back on," Lexa said and Rick turned to Marshall.

"What do you think?" he asked and the ghost

didn't answer. His red eyes were thoughtful and he was rubbing his chin.

"I don't know what to think Rick—it could be anything," the spirit replied.

"Well, do you think it's another phantom or what?" Rick asked and again the ghost was silent.

"Rick to be completely and upsettingly honest—I'd need to talk to them myself . . . I'm not quite sure," the ghoul's replied a few minutes later.

"Helpful aren't we? Well, let's start watching and maybe we'll get another IM," Kari said as Lexa pulled out "Legally Blonde." She popped it in and they all stared at the screen. Instead of playing the movie, the screen went black and the lights in the room went out. The electronics in the room started to go haywire, a girl's face came up on the screen. Her eyes were blank and staring and her skin was deathly pale.

"Help me . . ." she whispered and then everything came back on.

"What was that?" Lexa asked and Rick shook his head open mouthed as Kari shivered slightly.

"I . . . I have no idea," Rick said and they all looked up at Marshall who was looking at the screen.

"I don't know for sure, but I think we might be dealing with a demon. I'm not sure—either that or some kind of analytical zombie," Marshall said and laughed a hollow laugh that was more sarcastic than anything.

"No time for jokes, Marshall," Rick gulped. This was one that they hadn't dealt with before.

"Reminded me of 'The Ring' . . . that girl . . . on the TV," Lexa said.

"It did a little, but it was just deathly pale and the hair wasn't long and black, it was up in a pony tail and brown," Kari said logically.

"Does 'it' have a name?" Rick asked.

"I don't know . . . we'll have to ask it," Marshall said as they played the movie.

"No jokes, Marshall please," Rick groaned.

"Okay, okay . . ." Marshall smiled. He floated above their heads, cross legged, with his arms folded.

Later that night they were half way through "LOTR Return of the King" and it paused to show a message.

"Help me," it read.

"We're trying to," Marshall said out loud before Rick could reach the keyboard. It appeared on the screen as he said it.

"Who is this?" they replied.

"Colonial James C. Marshall," Marshall replied.

"Hello, you are not who I want though," the reply came through.

"I am replying for who you want . . . what is your name?" Marshall asked.

"My name is Rose Ta—," the reply stopped as the connection was broken when the sender signed off again.

"Rose Ta . . . Taylor," Kari said as the movie started again.

"Maybe . . . I'll look it up." Rick stood up and walked over to his computer. A few minutes later he sat back down.

"Nothing—I guess we just have to wait," Rick said.

SOMETHING

Rick woke up early. It was a week after his first encounter with the unknown sender and apparently they had given up.

"Good morning, Marshall," Rick said and Marshall nodded thoughtfully. He had been thinking a lot since their last encounter and had disappeared on several occasions to go see something.

"Morning, Captain," Marshall yawned.

"Any messages?" Rick asked and the ghoul yawned.

"Not a single one," the phantom replied. Rick walked over to his computer and looked at the screen. It was blank, devoid of messages, the screen was a star field. He pulled on his jeans and t-shirt then grabbed his backpack. He sped up the stairs and walked into the kitchen, kissed his mom on the cheek, grabbed an apple, waved at his dad and ran out the door. He ran down the street and just barely caught the bus. He walked down the aisle and sat down next to Kari; Lexa lived in another part of the neighborhood and took a different bus.

"Any messages from your phantom friend?" the girl asked as he began to eat the apple, he shook his head as the bus stopped again to allow more people on. Ryu walked back and sat down, squashing Rick into Kari who just moved and sat on Rick's lap.

"Who said you could sit there?" Rick asked.

"No one," she smiled. She was wearing a pair of loose tan capris and a tight blue shirt; the sleeves were down to her elbows. A silver charm bracelet was on her wrist.

"Okay, and you figure its okay no matter what?" Rick asked and she smiled and nodded. Her hair was up in double buns again with navy blue chopsticks through them.

"Pretty much—you don't seem to have a problem with it," Kari laughed at him.

"I don't think he does," Ryu laughed. The bus stopped again and more people got on.

"It's never normally this packed," Kari said to Ryu and Rick.

"Who knows? Maybe it's just your imagination—you have a very vivid one," Ryu told her and Rick laughed.

"No I'm serious," she said as they finally arrived at the school.

"Rick, when are you getting that car?" Ryu complained.

"Whenever it's my 17th birthday," Rick replied. They got off the bus as the bell rang and walked into the school building.

"Good morning . . . people . . . ," Lexa laughed after thinking about it.

"You are so blonde," her best friend told her.

"Thank you and you are so knobby," she told Kari.

"I don't know whether that was an insult or a compliment," Kari laughed.

"Don't look at us."

The boys shrugged. Lexa was wearing a layered skirt and a tight white top that read, 'Drama Queen.'

"Look here comes ugly, uglier and ugliest," Rick said as three girls walked by. They were Areos just as much as Lexa and Kari; they just were considered the most popular.

"I know what you mean. Didn't you go out with ugliest?" Ryu asked out loud just as they walked by.

"Yeah, what a mistake, that was a few years ago though," he replied as the girls stopped.

"What was that—half-breed?" she asked him. Rick walked in front of him.

"Excuse me, who were you talking to?" Rick asked. He was the only full fledged Areos in the school and everyone knew him. All the others were half-breeds. "As I remember Flannery, your mother is an elf, making you a half breed as well, so I wouldn't be talking," Rick said calmly.

"You . . . you stupid . . ." Flannery huffed and walked off.

"Wow, thanks, I thought I was going to be blasted into next week."

"She wouldn't dare attack you," Rick replied. Lexa smiled.

"Good ol' Rick, he'll never let us down." She smiled. Rick nodded.

"Come on, we're going to be late," Ryu said and he and Kari walked to English while Rick and Lexa walked to History.

"*Rick! Rick—*," Rick heard Marshall's voice in his head and looked around.

"What is it?" Rick asked him and what Marshall said next surprised him.

"*We're dealing with a siren.*" Marshall's voice said.

"A siren?"

"*Well something of the sort . . . it's actually called a mirror*," Marshall told him.

"I have History—let's talk about this when I get home." Rick blocked the phantom out and continued to do his work.

Later that night Rick was sitting at his desk when his phone rang.

"Great not another, 'you're going to die in seven days' thing," Rick sighed and answered, "Hello."

"Will you help me?" Rick heard a faint and fuzzy voice.

"Who is this?" he asked and the noise of a phone breaking up came through. "Hello?"

"Help me please . . . help . . ." the small voice said and the phone broke up again.

"Who is this?" he asked and her image appeared on the screen of his TV. His computer was going haywire again and he dropped his phone. "DAD!" Rick called and his father came down the stairs.

"Rick what is . . ." he saw the girl on the TV, "OUT OF MY HOUSE! FOUL SPIRIT OF DARKNESS, MIRROR NOT YOUR PAIN!" His father bellowed and the room returned to normal as Rick stood up, shaken to the core.

"What was that thing?" Rick asked.

"I told you, it's a mirror," Marshall said.

"Explain," Rick's father inquired simply.

"I don't know I just got this strange phone call and then that thing came up on my TV. It wants my help."

"A mirror asking for help; that's a new one," his father said thoughtfully.

"I want to help her, Dad, just let me try," Rick pleaded and his father sighed.

"Remember that spell, you might need it," he sighed and Rick smiled.

"Thanks." He smiled and his father walked up the stairs.

"Come on please be there, be there, be there—please . . ." Rick said as Kari's phone rang.

"Hello?" came her reply.

"It's back," Rick said and she gasped.

"What does it want now?" she asked him.

"I don't know. I think she still wants my help but how should I know?" Rick asked as he paced back and forth in his room.

"You sound scared. Do you want us to come over?" she asked.

"Who's us?" he asked and heard Lexa laugh.

"Who else silly?" she asked him and he laughed.

"Sure, I guess," he said to her.

"Maybe I should stay at my house—do some research on who she is. We can use messaging and phones to keep in touch," Lexa told them.

"Okay. I'll meet you at your house in a few minutes," Kari said and hung up.

"So, do you know her name?" Lexa asked.

"Nothing but what she told me the other day. I looked up 'mirrors' in my book and it said that they were dead spirits that were turned into demons. They will try to get you to die the same way that *they* did but this one is different. It seems to have a purpose; almost like she wants us to really help her," Rick said and the door bell rang. "That was fast," he said and ran up the stairs.

"Hello, Mr. Daniels, how are you today?" he heard Kari's voice.

"I knew one of you was going to be coming," he heard his father say and Kari walked down the stairs.

"So anything else?" Lexa asked, she was on speaker phone.

"No Lexa, now be quiet," Rick said and he and Kari sat down at his computer.

"What was her name again?" Lexa asked and Rick thought about it.

"Rose something . . ." Rick replied.

"I think I may have found something," Lexa said excitedly.

THE LIES

"You found something?" Kari asked.

"I think so . . . I'm not sure," Lexa replied. She was sitting on her bed, her pink laptop in her lap. She had bought one like the one Reese Witherspoon's character owned in "Legally Blonde" after falling in love with it. Her blonde hair was up in a loose bun at the back of her head. She was chewing on the end of a black ink pen. Her headset was just as pink as her lap top, as was her phone. She was wearing blue jeans that had been rolled up again to her calves and she had on a black tank top with a pink and orange light jacket over the top.

"*What do you mean you're not sure?*" Kari's voice came over the line curiously.

"I don't know, but it says here that about eighty years ago a ship sunk in the Bermuda Triangle. On the passenger list was someone named Rose Tarsal," Lexa said.

"*It could be someone else—there are a lot of people named Rose out there*," Kari said to her.

"She was on the passenger list but they never found her body . . . they don't know what happened to her," Lexa added, reading off the information.

"Who knows . . . it could be . . . ," Rick told Kari.

"*Hey there's more. Although Rose was not discovered, her parents were rescued safe and sound. One witness says, 'They didn't seem to be too upset that their daughter was onboard the sinking ship . . . when I asked them about it they said that it wasn't good to hold on to the past.' Another witness said that he had seen the couple and their daughter onboard and they seemed like a happy family.* Lexa wondered aloud, *Was there something more to this family than meets the eye?"*

"Okay that's a little bit creepy," Kari said.

"*I don't know about you guys but I'm smelling something very fishy—are you?"* Lexa asked.

"*Yeah, I know what you mean . . . why a seemingly happy set of parents who seemingly loved their child would not care that she was slowly sinking to the bottom of the ocean?"* Lexa asked.

"Who knows?" Kari said out loud.

"*There's another bit . . .*" Lexa clicked down to see the rest of the article. "*By Ra . . . listen to this . . . the only thing they found of the girl was her pet dog. It was found struggling to stay afloat on top of a suitcase. It was whining and crying but the suitcase and the dog sank before they could rescue it.*" Lexa's heart began to race, she was scared now of what was going on.

"Guys, this is starting to get really creepy," Lexa said softly.

"I know but the question is—what *is* going on?" Rick asked them.

"How should we know?" Lexa replied.

"Yeah, it's your spook," Kari said to him.

Rick gulped.

"That's what scares me," Marshall said. The usually good natured haunt looked pale.

"Guys . . ." Lexa cried as suddenly everything in her room shut off. Her room was completely dark and her laptop was leaking water.

"Will you help me?"

Lexa heard the girl's voice. It was distorted and shaky. A crackling sound come over the line and Lexa heard water and her laptop began to leak water again as the girl's face appeared on the screen—only this time she was with a dog who resembled Lassie.

"I . . . I can try . . . ," Lexa said, fear glowing in her eyes.

"Come with me . . . ," the haunt said and Lexa shook her head.

"Not yet . . . I will someday . . . I promise." Lexa shuddered as the girl disappeared and everything came back on in her room.

The phone was dead on the other line and Kari and Rick exchanged looks. He hung up and on the computer screen there was a message.

"Will you help me?" it read.

"We're trying . . . ," Rick said.

"Help me . . . ," the girl signed off.

"What does she want us to do?" Kari asked Rick and he shrugged.

"How should I know . . . maybe she wants us to find her dog?" His phone rang and he put it on speakerphone.

"G-guys—I'm c-coming o-over." They heard Lexa on the other line then she hung up. Kari was sitting there in the clothes she was wearing earlier, looking like a lost puppy.

"What was that about?" Marshall asked them and Rick shrugged.

"I don't know, Marshall—I really don't, but she sounded really scared," Rick replied.

"Marshall, do you know about all this?" Kari asked the apparition.

"No, I've never heard of any of it . . . remember I died in 1867. I don't know much," Marshall replied to the girl.

"Hold on I have an idea," Rick said and turned to his desktop. He typed something into his computer. "Yeah here it is, this site is for people to tell their true stories about ghosts," Rick said. "I looked up Rose's file. There have been over a hundred sightings of her but none as extensive as ours," Rick said and Kari moved over to gaze over his shoulder.

"Look, someone has a picture of her from fifty years ago." Kari pointed one of her fingers at the screen, her other hand on Rick's shoulder.

"Guys . . ." Lexa came walking down the stairs, her pink laptop in her arms. She looked terrified.

"What's wrong?" Rick asked her as she walked stiffly over to them.

"The girl . . . the girl . . . she's . . . she's . . . she came to my house . . . she talked to me . . . she wants to show me something . . . she wants to show it to me . . . ," Lexa said as she sat down, shaking with fear. Rick put his arm around Lexa's shoulders.

"Calm down . . . Lexa you're talking nonsense . . . now what?" Rick asked and she took in a deep breath then jumped as there was a knock at Rick's window. Ryu climbed down.

"Regular party down here, eh?" Ryu asked, his navy blue laptop in his arm.

"You moron, why did you do that?" Kari asked.

"I don't know I'm sorry, Rick messaged me and told me to come over and to bring my laptop," Ryu shrugged.

"I did—I'm sorry he scared you, Lexa," Rick told the frightened girl. He flipped his brown hair out of his face by shaking his head.

"So what's up?" Ryu asked as he opened his computer.

"We're doing research on the girl . . . I thought we could use our ghost specialist to help," Rick said.

"Ah, I see I don't count any more?" Marshall asked and they all laughed, even Lexa laughed weakly.

"Are you calm enough to talk yet?" Rick asked her.

"The girl, Rose, she came, she was on my laptop, and my phone . . . she was talking to me. She wants to show me something but I don't want to see it," Lexa told him.

"She wants to show you something?" Rick asked and she nodded.

"I don't know why I didn't go but I remembered what you had said so I didn't go . . . ," Lexa said. "I'm okay now . . . I just was scared of her . . . let's keep looking things up; there has to be more," she said and opened her laptop.

"What are we looking for?" Ryu asked them.

"Anything on Rose Tarsal," Kari replied—she was on Rick's laptop and he was on the desktop.

"Anything on Rose Tarsal . . . I've heard that name before . . . oh yeah . . . wasn't she the one in the suitcase?" Ryu asked thoughtfully.

"What did you say?" Kari asked him.

"Well there was this movie I saw and there was this little girl in it and her name was Rose Tarsal, she ended up in a suitcase at the end . . . it was really sad," Ryu told them

"A suitcase?" Rick repeated. "I remember that now, you and I saw it together, it was called like . . . "Bermuda" right?" Rick asked and Ryu nodded.

"She ended up in a suitcase . . . ," Kari repeated.

"I remember that movie. I saw it with my dad. He hated going to watch mortal movies until I took him to see that," Lexa laughed.

"Come on . . . stop with the movie and look for stuff on her," Ryu said and they all turned back to their computers.

About The Parents

It was getting into the wee hours of the morning. Kari had fallen asleep on Rick's shoulder. They were sitting on the futon. He and Ryu were the only one's awake; Lexa was asleep with her head on Ryu's thigh. Her pink computer was still open and glowing. Kari's open laptop was still in her lap, she was sitting cross legged next to Rick. The glow of Rick and Ryu's laptops were the only things lighting the room as Ryu shut Lexa's computer.

"Anything?" Ryu asked quietly.

"Nothing yet. It's all about the boat and different speculations on what caused the crash and there's a brief mention of her name," Rick replied.

"I think I found something but it's about her parents not her . . . but, maybe if we learn about her parents we can learn more about her," Ryu suggested.

"What did you find?" Rick asked across the room.

"Listen to this: Mr. and Mrs. Darrel Tarsal adopted a child, her parents died in a fire that destroyed their home. They named her Rose after her adopted grandmother. The wealthy couple disinclined to respond to our questioning on how they found the girl. Her original name was Darla Jackal and her parents were from Africa. Mrs. Sylvia Tarsal was hesitant to tell us even this so we have reason to suspect that they have something to hide." Ryu read. Across the room and Marshall looked thoughtful.

"I knew Rose Tarsal. She was a very prominent young woman when I was alive. Yes, she came overseas to the United States in 1846 . . . I remember that day . . . I saw her off you know."

"I thought you said . . ."

"I said I don't know Darla Jackal but I *do* know Rose Tarsal Sr." the phantom told him.

"Okay then. What can you tell us about Rose and her family?" Ryu asked the ghost.

"Rose was born to rich parents in 1828. I was born in 1821. Rose was beautiful even as a child. Her father died when she was 17 and her mother decided to move to the United States. She was 19 when she left. I heard she had a son with some man named Tarsal and that was the last I remember before I died," Marshall told them.

"Let's look up more stuff on Mr. and Mrs. Darrel Tarsal," Ryu said and Rick nodded. They worked for hours on end, it was 6 o'clock when they stopped their search out of fatigue.

"Ryu, I can't work any more I need sleep," Rick sighed, resting his head on Kari's shoulder Ryu nodded sleepily and leaned his head back on the wall. While they were sleeping Marshall was still searching on their computers. He was sitting there in the middle of the air, cross legged and with his arms folded across his chest.

"Rick?" Marshall heard Rick's father's voice.

"Atem, he's gone . . . but I need to ask you a few questions." the specter said.

"What is it James?" Atem asked walking down and leaning his arms on the railing of the stairs.

"What do you know about Isabel Jackal?" Marshall asked him.

"Isabel? She was a lovely woman. I remember meeting her a few months before she died in that fire, remember that?" Atem asked the spirit and he nodded.

"I was trapped so how could I not?" Marshall said.

"Why do you want to know?" Atem asked his friend.

"Because her daughter is the mirror. She was adopted at a young age after the fire but the Tarsal's . . . I don't know what went wrong," Marshall said.

"Neither do I, but why would her adopted parents not care that their daughter was sinking to the bottom of the ocean?" Atem asked the phantom.

"I don't know, but I'm going to help these kids find out. Oh, and Atem . . . ," the specter said as Atem turned to leave.

"Yes, James?" Atem asked.

"Don't step there," the ghost said pointing to a crack where Atem's foot was about to hit.

"Thank you James," Atem said then walked up the stairs, closing the door.

A few hours later Rick woke up as Kari moved her head. He jolted up straight looking at his computer. On it was a picture of the Tarsal family.

"How . . . ?" Rick asked the phantom as Kari woke up.

"What is that?" she asked him pointing at the screen.

"It's the Tarsals," Rick yawned.

"I was looking while you were asleep," Marshall said pointing at the black laptop.

"Thanks, Marshall," Rick said as Kari stretched.

"Are we going to be doing this all day or can we get out into the sun a bit?" Lexa asked them all as she woke up, waking Ryu with her.

"I think some sun will do us all some good. Take our minds off this for a bit," Rick nodded. "Let's all meet at the beach in 30 minutes," Rick said and Lexa looked scared.

"Should we really be separated like that?" she asked and Kari looked at her.

"I'll come with you," Kari told her and stood

up. The girls walked up the stairs, leaving their computers there.

"I'll protect you," Ryu laughed.

"No, I think it'll probably be me doing the protecting," He replied. Ryu was already in his swim trunks so Rick walked into the bathroom to change. He finished and looked into the mirror. He had an odd idea. If mirrors reflected anything, maybe they could get the mirror herself to show them what happened. Then he remembered what the girl had said to Lexa . . . she had wanted to show her something . . . but what? Marshall appeared behind him scaring him to death.

"Marshall, watch it—you scared me," Rick told the phantasm.

"Sorry, Captain didn't mean to," Marshall chortled.

"Sure you didn't," the young man replied.

"I'm serious. So, have you figured anything else out yet?" the mischievous spirit asked him.

"What have you got up your sleeve?" Rick asked him.

"Nothing, see," the ghost said honestly, pulling his sleeves down at the wrist for him to see.

"You know what I mean you pest," Rick grumbled.

"All right, all right—listen here. I can contact the spirit of Isabelle Jackal. I know her and I think she might be able to shine some light on her daughter," the shadow said, his strong face thoughtful.

"When?" Rick asked.

"Tonight—I can ask her to come over. You guys go have fun at the beach," the phantom said and faded off as Rick opened the door.

"Marshall is going to talk to Isabelle Jackal, Darla's mother," Rick told Ryu who looked up.

"Really? Hmm I wonder how that will go . . . ," Ryu laughed as the two of them walked out, Rick threw Ryu his surf board as he grabbed his.

"Dude." They laughed together making fun of the surfer stereotype as they walked off towards the beach.

A Day at the Beach

The girls were already out there when they arrived. Kari was in a shimmering silver bikini with a wet suit hanging from her hips and Lexa in a bright incandescent pink bathing suit, also with a wet suit on. They were standing with their boards waiting. Rick smiled as he walked over. Both he and Ryu had put wet suits on and they all matched.

"Well, aren't we the quadruplets?" he laughed, leaning on his board slightly.

"I know look at the waves," Lexa smiled as Kari pulled her wet suit up to put it on. Rick zipped up the back for her.

"They look like fun," Ryu laughed. People were already out surfing in the cold waters.

"Well, what are we sitting here for?" Kari laughed and ran out, carrying her board. She put it in the water, flopped onto it and began to swim out as every one else followed.

"Slice and dice!" Kari called out as she and her board came out the top of the rolling wave and flipped over, landing on the top, she slid her foot slightly to the nose and slid back into the wave. She skimmed over the inside as finally the wave crashed. She went under and came back up.

"Nice!" Lexa called out to her friend as they swam back out. Rick caught the next one and sailed into the air.

"Higher flier!" he called back to Kari. He cut through the water as if it were butter. He cut Ryu off as he sailed into the wave. Rick slid his hand along the inside of the rolling wave then flew back up through the top of the wave, flying into the sky before turning and finally being sucked under as the wave crashed.

"How do you do that?" Lexa asked Rick as he swam over to them. The Higher Flier was his signature move. They all had one and no one else could do the move like them.

"I don't know—let's see you then," Rick said to the girl.

"Fine." She swam out and caught the next wave. She slid easily through the wave, zigzagging through the current. Then she flew out the top and came back down except she and her board were moving backwards. "Magic Moonwalk!" she yelled at him as she swam up to him.

"All right, you saved the best for last," Ryu laughed. He swam out. But he didn't ride the first wave or second then a huge one rose over him and he smiled blazing through the water to the top. He shredded back down, riding low to the board as he spun back up through the back of the wave, spinning so he was on the back of it then slid down the front again.

"I love it when he does this," Lexa smiled.

"It is pretty cool isn't it?" Rick laughed. Ryu, with a determined look on his face rode straight up the wave as it curled, going into a spiraling motion.

"Disappearing Act!" he yelled at them as the spiraling board and rider disappeared under the water and the wave crashed. But he didn't come back up.

"Where'd he go?" Kari asked, holding her hands to her mouth. Ryu's soggy head came back above the water.

"That was a bit more of a Scaring Act, Ryu; these girls go into total fright mode when you don't come up. Even though they've seen you do it hundreds of times it still scares them," Rick said and the girls turned in to tan while Ryu and Rick went back out to surf.

"Well, that was fun," Kari said as they dried off and laid out on the beach chairs.

"Yeah, aren't the guys great?" Lexa asked and Kari nodded.

"So, does he know that you like him yet?" Kari asked back.

"You shut up before he hears you!" Lexa giggled.

"Yeah, right. Like he's going to hear me say, 'Lexa likes Ryu.' I think he already knows anyway," Kari told her.

"How would he know?" Lexa asked and Kari looked off the other way innocently. "YOU TOLD HIM!" she cried.

"It just sorta slipped out . . . I mean . . . he likes you, too . . ." Kari told her.

"I will never know who you like because you won't tell me," Lexa said to her friend.

"Lexa, you know why I won't tell you?" Kari asked.

"No . . ."

"Because if I told you . . . you would tell him the way I told Ryu," Kari said to her.

"No, I wouldn't," Lexa said.

"Yeah . . . yeah, you would," Kari told her and laid back to tan.

Rick shredded through the waves and Ryu cut him off.

"What was that for?" Rick asked as they both flew into the air and spun. Landing on the top of the wave then sliding back down, Ryu began to spiral again, Rick following him.

"Payback for earlier!" Ryu called back over his shoulder then looked around. Rick was no where in sight, then he looked up and Rick was upside down above him. He slid back down to the other side.

"I guess I deserved it," Rick replied.

"I guess you did," Ryu laughed as the waved crashed and they were left sitting on their boards as the small waves came.

"So, is it true you're going to ask Lexa out?" Rick asked with an odd smile on his face.

"Where did you hear that?" Ryu asked his friend.

"I see the way you look at her you idiot . . . I'm not stupid."

"Oh, you could have fooled me," Ryu sang then ducked as Rick tried to grab him.

"Thanks . . . this is for that." Rick caught Ryu's head under his arms, rubbing his knuckles into his already messed up silver hair.

"You got something to hold that mess out of your face I see," Ryu said pointing to the sunglasses on the top of Rick's head.

"Yeah, other wise I wouldn't have any eyes," Rick said running his hand through his spiky mess of brown hair.

"So, is it true about you and Kari?" Ryu asked, " . . . while we're on the subject," He smirked.

"It depends—what do you mean?" Rick asked him and Ryu splashed him with water.

"Come on mate tell me," the Australian said.

"Tell *me* what *you* mean," Rick said and Ryu splashed him again.

"You know what I mean. Are you going to or are you not going to ask Kari out, mate . . . she's fine," Ryu told him.

"You answer me and I'll tell you," the American said back.

"Oh, you are a cheek, come here and take what's coming to you!" the Aussie cried and swam after Rick who was getting closer to shore. Rick ran up, stuck the end of his board in the ground and before he could run, Ryu slammed into him from the side.

"Get off!" Rick cried, pushed him away and ran off down the beach again with Ryu close on his heels. The girls watched as once again Ryu made a flying tackle and slammed Rick to the ground, this time landing with his face directly in front of his.

"I'm not going to tell," Rick laughed.

"I'm going to make you tell," Ryu said pinning his arms and legs to the ground with his own.

"No, Ryu get off!"

"Tell me mate and I will.," the Aussie insisted and Rick sighed.

"All right, I was thinking about it. Happy now?" Rick asked him as Ryu let him up. Rick dusted himself off and frowned at Ryu. "You have to tell me now," he said evilly and the smaller boy took off down the beach. It was easier for Rick to get him down. He landed with his hands on Ryu's shoulders and his knees on his thighs.

"Tell me . . ." he said. The silver haired boy wriggled uselessly to try and get free.

"YES! FINE, YES! NOW GET YOUR BLOODY KNEE OUT OF MY CROTCH!" Ryu yelled and Rick let him up.

"Are you two quite done yet?" the girls asked them.

"I am, but I think Ryu here could use a hand," Rick laughed as Lexa helped the smaller boy up.

"Why were you two doing that any way?" Kari asked Ryu who laughed and coughed up a bit of sand.

"Nitty gritties . . . don't you gals worry now . . . we're as okay as we can get," Ryu said to them.

"Come on, we still have more day left," Rick said and they ran out into the waves.

ISABELLE JACKAL

Kari ran into her room and her puppy barked at her happily. She pulled off her sandy clothes and turned on the shower.

"All right . . . all right, Pooch hold on," she said to the impatient Husky. It was black and white with brilliant blue eyes. Rick had seen it and had called it Pooch and it had stuck so the dog thought its name was Pooch which was cute but she thought it was ridiculous. She got in the shower, the hot water cleansing her as she shampooed her hair. She was thinking about Rick again Kari realized . . . she couldn't figure why he was so fun to be around, but he was. She scrubbed and sand fell from her scalp. Her long silky almost black hair hung down around her waist, no one ever saw it down. She thought it a nuisance. Everyone asked her why she just didn't cut it off and she would always answer them with one answer:

"I'm waiting for Rick to tell me to cut it," she said out loud. She closed her eyes as she rinsed the conditioner out. She turned off the tap and walked into her bathroom. Wrapping a towel around herself she looked up and screamed. In the mirror was the girl. She was pale and deathly white. Her hair was light brown and her blank blue eyes were boring into hers.

"Will you help me?" her voice was stronger this time.

"I'm trying . . . I'm trying . . ." Kari gasped, it felt as though the room was closing in on her.

"Thank you . . ."

She heard the girl's voice and saw that next to her was the lassie dog.

"Please, will you tell me what happened?" Kari asked the girl. "Darla, will you tell me?" she asked calling her by her real name.

"What . . . what did you call me?" the specter asked.

"That's your real name . . . isn't it?" Kari asked and the girl's face suddenly was gone. Kari screamed again as the girl began to show her images, blurry speeding images that were so fast she barely caught most of them. When it ended, Kari fell to the floor, unconscious.

Kari woke a few hours later and she looked around. She was in her bathroom but there was someone beside her.

"Decided to take a nap, eh?" she heard Rick's voice.

"Rick . . . she was here . . . she came here in my mirror . . . she talked to me and showed me something," she said as he helped her to her feet. She clutched the towel around herself.

"Why do you always have your hair up? It's so pretty down," Rick said running one of her soft locks through his fingers.

"I'll think about it, now get. I need to dress," she said and shooed him out of her bathroom. She pulled on a pair of jeans and rolled the bottoms up like Lexa did and pulled on her shirt which was a tight shirt like her navy blue one she had worn during testing day. Her charm bracelet was still on her wrist and as she walked out, she left her hair down, mostly. She had braided it into a long dark braid. She slipped on her shoes and followed Rick out the door after putting her puppy's leash on and locking the door. Her parents were out shopping.

"Isn't it your birthday in a week?" Rick asked her as they walked.

"Yeah . . . why?" she asked him and he smiled.

"I thought maybe you'd let me take you out for your birthday next week," Rick asked, keeping his face straight ahead as he looked at her out of the corner of his eye. She smirked.

"Is that a date then?" she asked him. Pooch hopped up his leg trying to get him to pay attention to him.

"I don't know . . . do you want it to be?" Rick asked her back.

"Maybe . . ." she smiled. He laughed and petted the dog.

"All right . . . all right Pooch, I'll pay attention to you," Rick said as he picked the puppy up. It licked his face and neck. "I think I just French kissed your dog," Rick said making a face.

"That's why you shouldn't smile when you're holding him," Kari smiled as they arrived at his house.

"We're here," Rick said as they walked down the stairs and Lexa and Ryu looked up. Rick raised his eyebrows when he saw Ryu's arm around her shoulders.

"Leave it mate . . . leave it alone," he said to Rick.

"All right, whatever," he said and turned around as the lights went out. Marshall came out leading a pretty woman in an old fashioned dress. She was in evening attire and her hair was up in a bun at the back of her head.

"Fellows . . . my good friends . . . meet Isabelle Jackal," Marshall said and bowed.

"Well, hello there." Isabelle had a soft motherly voice and a fan in her hand.

"Hello . . . look . . . may we ask you a few

questions about your daughter?" Kari asked and she turned to her.

"What a strange girl. Why are you wearing men's clothes?" Isabelle asked.

"It's our fashion now . . . but, can you tell us some things about Darla?" Kari asked and Isabelle nodded. They all sat down—well, the living ones. Isabelle sat down in a wooden chair, or rather floated above a real wooden chair, her back perfectly straight. Marshall just sat in the middle of the air cross- legged and with his arms folded across his chest once again. Pooch walked over to the woman and tried to jump up in her lap but instead fell through her and she laughed.

"What would you like to know?" the woman asked them.

"First, I have a question—that is if Kari will let me interrupt," Rick said and Kari nodded.

"Yes? What is your name?"

"Rick. Why did your house catch on fire?" Rick asked and he got the reaction he wanted . . . disgust.

"It didn't light itself, Rick—someone lit it," Isabelle's tone grew dark. "Someone fiendish and horrible enough to kill myself and my husband to get our daughter," Isabelle said to them.

"Why did they want your daughter?" Kari asked softly.

"Kari, is it not? That's a pretty oriental name.

They wanted Darla because she was special . . . she had a gift of shape shifting; she was a 'metamorph.' This person wanted her because her body produced a serum that could shift other things as well, and he was going to use it for military purposes." Isabelle said softly.

"Why would anyone do such a horrible thing?" Lexa asked.

"Because they were greedy and had no care for other's feelings," Marshall said.

"That will be quite enough, James," Isabelle said and the male phantom shut his mouth.

"Do you know what happened to your daughter?" Lexa asked her and she shook her graceful head.

"I have not seen my daughter since the day I died. I miss her dearly," Isabelle told them softly.

"That's why my parents named me Kari, 'beloved daughter of light.' Isabelle, I promise that we will do all we can to reunite you and your daughter but she wants us to do something, but I don't know what," Kari said, taking the ghost's hand.

"Kari, my dear, I do not know how to thank you," Isabelle responded.

"One question Kari—how are we going to . . . do this?" Everyone jumped at the quiet Australian's voice. He had been completely silent. "Mirrors only cross over when what they stayed for is accomplished," Ryu said to her.

"Ryu, that's it—oh, I love you!" Lexa gasped. Kari looked at her curiously as she kissed Ryu's lips then jumped off the bed. She ran over to her pink computer. She sat down and opened it.

"What's 'it'?" Isabelle asked as they all turned to look at her. Ryu was left in a complete daze.

"What he said—the only way that we can reunite you is by accomplishing what she wants us to do . . . so that's what we're going to do. We're going to ask her what she wants us to do," Lexa said hurriedly as she typed something in, "and then we're going to do it!"

"There's a problem with that as well. We never know when she's going to show up or how. So far we've had her in the TV, a laptop and a mirror. What's next? A suitcase?" Marshall asked and Rick's eyes lit up.

"Marshall . . . the suit case . . ." Kari grabbed her lime green computer and opened it. "The only thing they found of the girl was her pet dog. It was found struggling to stay afloat on top of a suitcase. It was whining and crying but the suitcase and the dog sank before they could rescue it," Rick read out loud to them.

"It's all starting to fall into place. Maybe Bermuda was right . . . maybe she is in the suitcase but, why would she be in there? Another question . . . how . . . ?" Rick said to them.

"I don't know. What significance does the dog have in all this?" Lexa asked.

"I don't know yet, but I swear I'm going to figure this out. We are going to figure this out together," Rick said.

"Oooohh—who's the manly leader?" Kari teased him.

"Kari, we can do this . . . we can . . . you know why we can?" Rick asked and they all shook their heads.

"Because friendship is stronger than hate and I have a feeling that extreme hate is going to play into this," Rick said.

"I will bet you anything that the dog knew that she was in that case and was trying to tell someone," Kari said.

Marshall leaned in close to Rick's ear. "I don't like taking from the hopelessly stupid but I'd take that bet," Marshall laughed.

"Dogs have a sense of smell that's very strong and they recognize their master's smell . . . maybe she smelled her master inside . . ." Kari said as her puppy hopped into her lap.

"I think you're on to something," Marshall said.

"All this excitement has made me faint. I will

come again to check and see how you are doing every once in a while. Good-bye friends." Isabelle smiled as she disappeared.

Puzzle Pieces

Rick was sitting on the floor while Kari laid on the futon over him. Ryu was sitting on the bed and next to him was Lexa. Kari was looking things up about the fire that Isabelle had mentioned. She wanted to know who started it.

"Rick hey—look at this," Kari said to him, tousling his already messy brown hair to get his attention.

"What?" he laughed and looked up at her.

"Look at the picture and listen to me read this," Kari said and he looked at the picture of a burnt-out building.

" 'The Jackal house burned, due to mysterious circumstances . . . there was an argument between family members and one is suspected of arson.' Now look at this picture." Kari pulled up a picture of a sullen faced man. " 'Damien Jackal is accused of arson and suspected of murder.' Now look at these two pictures next to each other." She clicked on another and a picture of a more clean shaven and dignified-looking man came up.

"They . . . they look the same," Rick said to her and she nodded.

"Rick, *this* man is Darrel Tarsal and *that* man is

Damien Jackal," Kari said tapping her index finger-nail on the screen of the computer.

"They're the same person," Rick said and Ryu and Lexa looked up.

"Damien Jackal and Darrel Tarsal are the same person. Okay, that's puzzle piece number one," Ryu said as Kari wrote it down.

"Now listen to this, 'Jackal is believed to be hiding out in an area not far from the homestead with the Jackal's baby girl, Darla,'" Kari said tapping her fingernail against the screen again. "I will bet you anything that Jackal burnt down the house to get Isabelle's daughter. Because, there's a bit more . . . 'Jackal was in the army before he was honorably discharged for medical reasons . . . he had pneumonia and back then they didn't know how to handle it so they just discharged him. He and his wife wanted children but couldn't have them and so he figured that what better thing to do than kill his brother and sister-in-law to get a baby. Then he learned . . . '"

"About her metamorphing powers and the serum it supplies and figured he could sell it to make money . . . I get it," Rick said and Ryu nodded.

"So he was going to travel to trade her serum, taking her and his wife with him. But, what the suit-case has to do with all this . . ." Ryu trailed off.

"We won't know until we meet again," Rick said and they all nodded.

"What we are going to do in the mean time is find out more about the sinking of the ship—what did it run into? How many people were on it and how many survived?—that can be you, Lexa. Ryu—start trying to find out the names of the people onboard and try to get a diagram of the ship. Rick—you try to find out more about Jackal's wife, what kind of family she came from and so forth. I'm going to try and figure out the rest of the story and get more information on Jackal himself," Kari said and they started working again.

A few hours later Rick looked up at the clock and stretched. It was 3 o'clock in the morning. He felt Kari tousle his hair.

"What is it?" he asked, turning around.

"Nothing, I just like to do that," Kari said sleepily tousling his hair again. She had her head resting on her right arm. Her computer was open in front of her. On it was an extensive paper on Damien Jackal. He turned to see Ryu and Lexa sound asleep.

"How long have they been that way?" he asked her.

"I don't know . . . a couple hours. You need some sleep, too—you look tired," Kari said, seeing the deep shadows under Rick's eyes. He yawned in reply.

"You all could use some sleep, you should stop obsessing over this case and get some rest," Marshall told the two. "I like their idea; sleep while you can, work when you can't," Marshall laughed.

"Marshall, we need to figure out . . . figure out . . ." Kari was resting her head on her arm and at the word sleep she was falling asleep. She tried another time to stay awake but a few minutes later she was sound asleep. Rick stood and walked over to the bed and pulled a blanket off. He covered the sleeping girl up, pulled off his shirt and lay back down on the floor. It was starting to get very hot in his down stairs room. He got back up and turned on the fan.

"She's gone; dead and gone," Marshall said looking at the sleeping Areos.

"Don't say that Marshall because then she will be—because you have the worst luck in the world. Although you're right, she's down for the count," Rick agreed laying back down in front of his computer.

"You should get some sleep trooper . . . have you looked in the mirror lately? I mean you have shadows under your eyes . . . ," Marshall said and Pooch walked over to Rick while growling at Kari's computer. Its hackles were raised and a deep low growl was rising in its throat.

"What's wrong Pooch?" Rick asked the puppy. The dog continued to growl and as Rick stared at Kari's computer screen he saw what it was looking at. It was another mirror but instead of it being Darla, it was Jackal. Remembering the spell his father had said. "FOUL SPIRIT OF DARKNESS, MIRROR NOT YOUR PAIN!" Rick shouted and the mirror disappeared but, the price was that he had woken the others.

"What were you shouting mate?" Ryu asked him seeing his friend's heaving chest.

" 'Foul spirit of darkness mirror not your pain'? Isn't that the vanishing spell for a mirror?" Kari yawned. She petted her puppy and the fox walked over and hopped into Rick's lap.

"I want to go back to my house and feed my cat," Lexa said. "Ryu, your cat is still occupying my backyard instead of yours," Lexa told him and he rolled his eyes.

"My cat likes you," he smiled.

"But, I don't want to go over there alone," Lexa said looking at Kari who raised her eyebrows at Ryu.

"Is there a look-link going on here?" Rick laughed.

"I'll come with you . . . we'll call you guys," Ryu said as they stood up and picked up their computers.

"Okay, te quiero mucho," Kari said, kissed air next to Lexa's cheek and she and Ryu left.

"What was that? I didn't know you spoke Spanish," Rick said to her and she shrugged.

"I didn't think you needed to know. Now, what were you yelling at?" she asked him as they both put their ear pieces on. Hers was her signature lime green color and his was the same brilliant blue as his computers.

"You won't believe this. Damien Jackal was on your computer screen. He was a mirror, like Darla," Rick replied.

"He was what? Gosh, are these things electronically oriented or what?" Kari said.

"You don't believe me do you?" Rick asked.

"It is a little unbelievable," she sighed.

"Might I cut in? I don't think he thinks it's unbelievable!" Marshall said pointing at the TV screen. There was a buzzing noise that sounded like a gunshot as Damien Jackal appeared on the screen.

"Not guilty . . . I told them . . . I didn't do it!" the apparition cried at them.

"You didn't burn the house down?"

"I would never do that. I know who it was, but they . . . they don't want us . . . want us . . ." the specter disappeared off the screen.

"He sounded hurried as if someone was after him," Kari said and there was a dark growl from behind them.

"I think we're playing with more than just this . . . I think there's a lot more to this story and I'm going to find out for Isabelle's sake," Marshall said.

"Marshall, do you think that there's someone that doesn't want these two to get through to us?" Rick asked the phantom and he nodded.

"Yes I do Rick . . . I do," the ghost replied darkly.

"Then why can we talk to Isabelle?" Kari asked. Her long braid falling into Rick's outstretched hand.

"Because she crossed over instead of staying on earth."

"Rick, let go of my hair," Kari laughed as he pulled the tie off her long silky hair, letting it fall around her shoulders.

"I did," he replied and smiled.

"You're a jerk," she laughed.

"You're still laughing," Rick replied.

A Speculation

It was two days later and they were still split up into two different houses. But this time the Areos were sound asleep. Kari was sitting on the futon with her computer next to her and Rick's head in her lap and his phone was next to her with her head-set plugged in and Lexa on the other line. They had told their parents that they were having a sleepover and just hanging out but for a few hours the day before Kari had been alone because Rick had gone to do something mysterious . . . some mystery trip to another part of town.

"Kari, do you know anything yet?" Lexa yawned into her mouth piece. Ryu was asleep next to her on her bed. She had her hair up in a bun at the back of her head and was wearing a light blue t-shirt with a jacket over it and a pair of rolled up jeans.

"No you?" Kari asked back, she was wearing a hoodie that read, 'Got Dance?' and a pair of tight jean capris. It was starting to cool off a little. It was around 60 degrees that day and it was still summer; an odd cooling trend for that time of year. Her hair was once again up in a braid and the tip was tied to the back of her head with a clip creating a loop.

An overnight bag was sitting on Rick's bed, full of clothes and shampoo and other things of that sort.

"Well, I think I found something but I'm not sure. You say that he said he wasn't guilty?" Lexa asked and Kari nodded on the other line.

"Yeah . . . why?" she asked gently running her fingers through Rick's messy hair.

"I found something on his trial," Lexa said clicking down the page.

"Hmmm . . . read it," she said. Then a message came up on her screen.

"Are you still helping me?" it read.

"Hey, I got an Instant Message from Darla—" Lexa could hear Kari's nails clicking on the keys as she typed.

"What'd she say?" Lexa asked.

"She wanted to know if we're still helping her and I told her, yes."

"You want to know what to do?" Darla asked.

"Yes please . . . please tell me," Kari said as she typed.

"I want you to find—," the girl logged off.

"She wants us to find something but she logged off before she could finish," Kari said.

"She wants us to find something . . . who knows," Marshall said to the Areos.

"Marshall I think she wants us to find out who really burnt down the house and I think that this man . . ."

Kari pointed to the picture of Darrel Tarsal, "might not be who we thought at first," Kari said tapping her fingernail on the screen.

"Is Rick still asleep?" Lexa asked.

"Yeah, he was pretty tired," Kari laughed. Rick moved in his sleep, turning over on his side.

"Sounds like it. I can hear him moving around; he always mumbles in his sleep," Lexa laughed.

"Yeah, he's taking me out to dinner tomorrow night for my birthday," Kari said and Lexa giggled.

"I always said you two would make a perfect couple," Lexa giggled quietly.

"Shhhh . . . we're not dating—he's just taking me out for dinner," Kari smiled.

"Yeah, that would be considered a date from my point of view," Lexa said to her best friend.

"Quiet . . . I know you're going to spread it around that we're going out, but unless he asks me, we're not," Kari said.

"Oooohh . . . does that mean that if he asks you, you'll say, yes?" Lexa asked softly.

"I . . . no! I mean . . . that's not it . . . I don't know what I'd say . . . I mean he is cute, but I mean . . ." Kari said stroking her fingers through his hair again.

"So, you would say yes . . . oh, so cute . . . ," Lexa sang on the other line.

"So . . . you and Ryu are a topic of discussion," Kari said, and as the girl's talked, the corners of Rick's mouth turned up in an unmistakable smile. He had been listening to the whole conversation; his earpiece was still in and was still connected to his phone which was in his pocket.

Rick opened his eyes and smiled up at Kari who jumped then laughed.

"What's wrong?" Lexa asked.

"Nothing, Rick scared me he just suddenly opened his eyes and looked up at me with the foggy blue eyes . . . it was kinda creepy," Kari laughed.

"Ow . . . my ear," he said putting his hand to his earpiece. Kari's eyes widened.

"Sounds like he heard our whole conversation," Lexa laughed and Ryu grumbled something at her.

"Hmmm . . . here dummy, put your earpiece on smart one," Lexa said and they heard a click as Ryu connected to their conversation.

"Morning mates," he said to them groggily.

"Good morning Ryu . . . sleep well?" Kari laughed.

"Very . . . except . . ." There was a noise of him spitting something out. "I have cat hair in my— what—Ow . . ." They heard a purr and Lexa laughed as there was a thud and then a bang resulting in a shout from Ryu.

"The cat just attacked him . . . well, he was

sitting unbalanced on the edge of the bed and the cat walked on him and he fell off and his laptop hit him in the face." Rick snorted a laugh as he sat up.

"Sounds like you've got a cat lover there," Rick laughed.

"Shut it, Rick," Ryu grouched.

"Well good morning, all," Marshall said as Lexa's web cam came up on Kari's screen.

"Shut it, Marshall," Ryu groaned and they could see Ryu rubbing his temples as he sat back down on Lexa's bed with his computer in his lap.

"So anything yet?" Ryu asked and Kari shook her head as her web cam turned on.

"Nothing, but I did find something on Damien's trial," Kari said taking a drink for the cappuccino that Rick's father had brought her.

"What?" Rick asked grabbing his lap top.

"Well, it's just a report from the investigation. They didn't investigate all the things that could have happened—they just figured that since he was there and he had Darla in his arms and Darla's parents were burning to death in a fire—there could have been other things that could have happened. Such as this." She clicked on something and then sent it to Lexa. "If you look to the side of this picture there is something we like to call a ghost . . . but instead. . . ." She clicked the person's face and the picture moved in to reveal the face of—

"Darrel Tarsal," Ryu gasped.

"Exactly. Listen to this: 'Darrel Tarsal . . . Jason Jackal's cousin had visited earlier that day and said that Jackal, who lived with his brother and sister-in-law, was very calm that day . . . he didn't know why Jackal would do something like this . . . so he and his wife adopted the Jackal's child. At the trial Jackal was mad with his damnation so much that he was screaming that he wasn't guilty. Jackal was hung four days later,'" Kari said clicking down.

"So Jackal is innocent, but then was it Tarsal?" Lexa asked.

"I don't know, but at the moment I think so," Rick said.

"There goes my theory on the army, Jackal was honorably discharged with pneumonia. But it wasn't him because he died a few weeks after Isabelle and her husband—hold on—," Kari said thoughtfully.

"What is it?"

"I've just thought of something," Kari said softly tapping her fingers on her laptop.

"Come on, Kari, tell us!" Ryu said.

"What if it wasn't Tarsal at the scene of the crime? What if . . . what if Isabelle's husband was disguised as Tarsal and the real Tarsal was in the fire?" Kari suggested.

"But Tarsal was just his cousin so how would they look so much alike?" Lexa asked.

"Genes—they might have had different parents but, one of his parents were related to the Jackals and that sullen look must run in the family," Rick said and Kari nodded.

"I have a few pictures of Jason Jackal. He looks exactly like his brother and cousin," Kari said clicking and sending the pictures to the others.

"Let's meet up and grab a bite . . . how about Johnny Rockets?" Ryu suggested and the girls nodded along with Rick.

"All right. I'll bring my computer and I'll show you this stuff," Kari said and the other two nodded and hung up.

A little while later they were sitting in a booth and Kari was drinking a soda with Lexa while the Areos ate at an amazing speed. A teen walked over to them in a pair of tattered jean shorts and a ripped blue shirt. She was called a 'Mithra,' a catlike humanoid. She looked like a human except she was covered in tan fur with seal points or her ears, paws and tail were a deep brown color. Her face was like a cat's cinched together and her nose was black with a spot on the tip in pink. Her tail was in much fascination to Kari's puppy. Her eyes were a mysterious blue color.

"Well, now if it isn't my Ghostbusters?" Tabitha asked.

"Hey Tabby what's up?" they asked the cat woman as she sat down.

"Nothing. You know how great it is to be cool once again?" the cat woman asked referring to the cool temperature. Her long chocolate brown hair was down past her knees and a pair of chocolate cat ears poked out of her head. She was thin and lean almost like a tiger and was as flexible as one.

"I hate the cold," Kari said.

"When you come from a small unknown island in Antarctica you tend to like the cold," the humanoid said. There were only a few of her kind still in existence because they were exiled to live in places that weren't suited for them. Although she looked young, Tabby was actually a few hundred years old—not unusual for the people on the island—which most people believed to be uninhabited.

"So, what have you been doing?"

"Babysitting," the cat woman replied, pointing at her humanoid parents with four little catlike children.

"Well, we've been trying to figure out something. I was wondering when you would come out because I have a question for you," Rick said.

"Yes?"

"What do you know about a boat sinking in the Bermuda Triangle about eighty years ago?" Rick asked.

"The one with the little girl and her parents? Oh, well, not much. All I know is that they never discovered her body and that her dog is still being seen all over the place," the cat said.

"WHOA! Rewind—what did you say?"

"They never discovered her body and her dog has been seen all over the place?" the cat said curiously, her ears sinking because she was afraid that she had said something wrong.

"You didn't do anything wrong—you've just helped us. Thank you, Tabby," Kari said as the cat walked out with her parents and the humanoid purred.

"Thank you! Call me if you need anything else!" she said.

"The dog . . ." they all said together.

AN UNWELCOME REVELATION

The next night Kari was in her room dressing for her birthday date. She had on a nice feathered black dress. It was held up by loose sleeves that hung to her hips. The top was up just a little below her collar bone the back hung down to the middle of her back. Her hair was down but on the left side of her head a decorated round clip held the loose bits to the side of her head, small ribbons hanging from it. Her eyes were outlined with black liner, bringing out the bright green color of her eyes. She grabbed her bag and walked down the stairs to answer the door as it rang. Her lime green cell phone was in her purse just in case Ryu and Lexa found anything.

"You look nice."

She smiled. Before her was Rick in a pair of jeans and a button shirt and sports jacket.

"I feel weird like this," he replied then waved a set of keys in front of her face. "Guess what I got early?" he asked and stepped back. The sleek deep black Mustang convertible was sitting in her driveway. She walked out completely amazed.

"You got it a month early?" Kari gasped.

"Look what else I have." He showed her his driver's license. "I've had my permit for six months meaning that I can drive without parents." He smiled and opened the side passenger door.

"Boy, you are just full of surprises tonight aren't you? So why did I have to dress up like this?" she asked him as they rode through the town.

"Because we're going to 'The Lotus' for your birthday," Rick told her and she looked at him with a wide-eyed 'are you serious?' look.

"Rick, are you joking?" she asked. 'The Lotus' was the most expensive restaurant in town and it was run by a chef from New York City. The food was delicious but, she hadn't been there since her parents' 15th anniversary when she was 14.

"Yes, I am. It's your sixteenth birthday tomorrow and you deserve a dinner for a 16 year old." Rick smiled as they parked in front of The Lotus.

"Rick I can't believe it . . . thank you. I mean not many guys take their best friends out for their birthdays to The Lotus," She said to him as he opened the door for her and escorted her into the restaurant.

"Daniels—party of two—reservations for eight o'clock," Rick said to the concierge who nodded and led them into the dining room.

"Have a nice meal. Your waiter will be with you in a moment" He said and walked back to the door.

"Okay, tell me how did you get a reservation to The Lotus?" Kari asked.

"I have friends in high places," he said as the owner and chef walked out from the back wiping his hands off.

"Rickie!" the man cried and walked over to shake the boy's hand.

"Hey Eric, what's going on?" Rick asked.

"I should be asking you the same question," the New Yorkian said looking at Kari.

"This is Kari, tomorrow's her 16th birthday—as I told you before," Rick said. Kari stood up and Eric took her hand and kissed the back of it.

"My congratulations to you my dear, you have a fine friend here who could talk the socks off a chicken." Eric smiled as the girl sat back down. Her wings had disappeared for the moment with a simple charm.

"So, what's on the menu?" Rick asked.

"You're waiter isn't here yet? He'll be out in a minute," Eric noted and then walked back into the kitchen.

"Odd friends you have Rick," Kari laughed.

"I don't know how I make them . . . I just do."

"You're an easy going guy and people love you," Kari said as a young man walked out to their table.

"Hey, David, what's up?" Rick asked shaking the boy's hand. David was a Dryad or something of a magic lineage. His family had moved to escape from the witch persecutions in England.

"Nothing much. Here's your menus," the young man said. "I will be back in a moment to take your order."

Rick nodded in thanks.

"It's so good to be able to sit with out that laptop or without having anything to do with Darla or Jackal," Rick sighed and then pulled something out of his pocket. "Happy birthday." He smiled and handed Kari a small box. Inside was a smooth silver ring and placed in the metal were jewels. In the middle was a diamond, larger than the rest, then two emeralds finally ending in sapphires.

"Rick . . . Rick how did you . . . ?" she asked slipping it on.

"How else, I saved money by doing everything I could around town to help out. I had it specially made, look inside," he said and she took the ring off looking inside the band.

"Happy Sweet Sixteen—From Rick," Kari read putting it back on. "Why?"

"Because I wanted to." Rick smiled.

"You are too cute you know that?" she asked looking at the ring.

"We're not engaged . . . I just bought you a ring . . ." he said.

"I know that, but I mean . . . aren't we just friends?" Kari asked mischievously.

"I don't know . . . do you want us to just be friends?" he asked.

'No!' her mind screamed. "I don't know . . . no . . . I don't . . . I don't Rick," Kari said softly.

"Well then . . . I wasn't expecting that," he replied as their lips moved closer together.

"OH MY GOSH!" Kari cried suddenly, breaking the moment.

"What?" Rick sighed.

"The serum, Rick, what if Jason Jackal used the serum from his daughter to make himself look exactly like Tarsal then burnt Tarsal and his wife, along with their home, to the ground? Damien Jackal though knew what was going on so that's why he tried to sneak away with Darla," Kari said excitedly.

"Why does Darla have to ruin *my* time?" Rick mumbled.

"Stop being such a spoiled sport," Kari scolded him and dragged him out to the car. "Please we can come back—please Rick. I want to do this—*please*," Kari begged, holding onto his hand.

He sighed. "Okay, but if you're not even partially right, I'm never going to try this again," Rick told her as he opened her car door. They drove away and Kari pulled out her cell phone.

"Well, that was fast. Did he try and kill you or did he just not show up?" Lexa asked.

"He's here but we're going home," Kari replied.

"Why? Did he take you to some place you don't like?"

"No, we went to The Lotus," Kari said and heard her scream.

"WHAT ARE YOU COMING BACK FOR, YOU MORON!?" Lexa yelled, Rick flinched, he could hear her from across the car.

"Because I have to. I hate to break it up . . . I mean its The Lotus and . . ."

"It's with Rick," Lexa said smoothly.

"Well, yes and no, but I swore to help Isabelle, so that's what I'm going to do," Kari said to her.

"Kari, I hope you know what you're doing—I mean he took you to *The Lotus* and you're turning that down to help a ghost?" Lexa said.

"Lexa, I know—but one dinner is not going to hurt . . . besides, I don't think this will be our last," Kari said and Rick almost ran into a mailbox out of surprise.

"All right, well call me when you get home," Lexa said and hung up.

"She was at Ryu's," Kari said to him as they pulled into her driveway. "I'll be right back down in a minute—this might be another all nighter," Kari said and ran up the stairs.

Rick leaned back in his seat. It had been so perfect. His night was going by without a hitch. It was just his luck to have the perfect moment and the perfect girl and then it turned the way he was dreading. He loved being around Kari and *with* her . . . it was just the way he was. He hoped that he might get that moment back someday.

"Hey," Kari said breathlessly as she got back in the car, her overnight bag in her hand along with her laptop case.

"You are something else," Rick told her.

"Thanks." She smiled.

As Long As My Heart Beats

When Rick and Kari arrived at his house Rick smiled as he saw Ryu and Lexa waving at them from the window.

"Hey! What's going on?" Ryu asked as they walked out.

"Well, we just came home from a dinner date that only *she* would ever interrupt to talk to a ghost," Rick replied.

"Wow, that's interesting—we've been researching Tarsal and his research. We'll tell you about it when we get inside," Ryu said as they walked in.

"You look so beautiful—why would you ever stop a date like that? Why would you break up any date with Rick?" Lexa asked.

"Because I promised to reunite Isabelle with her daughter and the only way I'm going to do it is by interrupting a little date."

"Little? LITTLE, ARE YOU NUTS?!? He took you to The Lotus and you're calling it—OH MY GOSH!" Lexa grabbed Kari's right hand, the ring was on her right ring finger. "He bought you this?" Lexa asked quietly as they walked down the stairs.

"Yeah," Kari said as they reached the bottom. She walked over to his bed and sighed. "Rick, you are the sloppiest person I know," she told him and began to make his bed. She finished and before they knew it she had cleaned his entire room within a matter of minutes.

"Okay, let me get this straight. He took you to The Lotus . . . then, you remembered something after he gives you a ring and then you left The Lotus? What in the world has gotten into you? No normal person would turn that down," Lexa said as Kari opened her laptop and searched for the serum.

"I'm not normal," Kari replied. She was still in her dress and she played with the fabric as she waited for the search to finish.

"Hey, you're back to normal!" Ryu laughed as Rick walked out of the bathroom, his sunglasses back on top of his head and his shirt and jacket in his hand. He hung them up and put his shoes away.

"I might need those again, I hope." Rick laughed and sat down next to the girls as Ryu did.

"Sex appeal much?" Lexa asked looking at Rick who's t-shirt was still in his hand.

"I'm working on it," he told her and pulled his shirt on.

"Oh Rick!" Marshall said floating through the wall. Isabelle followed.

"Hello—oh, you're dressed properly—did you throw all your men's clothes away?" Isabelle asked Kari who looked up.

"No, I still have them. Isabelle, I want to ask you a question. Who died in the fire with you?"

"My cousin-in-law—oh, he was such a kind and gentle man. He was investigating how . . ."

"How the metamorph serum could be used to heal deformed or injured people? Like people who were born without fingers or toes or were wounded and had limbs amputated. A more noble cause than what people had thought?" Lexa asked and Isabelle nodded.

"Exactly . . . exactly my dear, but see my husband thought it a useless task. He believed that we could develop the serum to be used as a chemical to infiltrate enemy lines," Isabelle said to them.

"So, you and Darrel Tarsal died in the fire together?" Rick asked.

"Yes, I remember the last thing he said to me. He said that he would see me on the other side," Isabelle's glazed eyes took on a faraway look.

"What about Darla?" Isabelle smiled at Kari.

"Damien took her, I told him that I didn't care about my own life as long as he got Darla out of there and took her far away, but they pinned this whole fire on him and Jason got away with my child."

"Is there something you'd like to tell us . . . like how Darla was actually by Damien?" Ryu said raising his eyebrows and if she could have, the phantom would have cried.

"Yes . . . I admit it. Damien and I . . . Darla was his daughter and unfortunately we couldn't tell Jason; he was too volatile. So we hid it from him and he believed that Darla was his, but he had a horrible temper and when he was frustrated he would . . . he would . . ." Suddenly to their surprise she just vanished.

"Marshall, what happened?" Kari asked the specter.

"She was interrupted. Someone or some thing doesn't want us to know the truth about Darla, but I think we're getting closer," Marshall said.

"Oooohh, do you have a thing for a certain ghost woman?" Rick teased the phantom.

"Maybe," Marshall smiled. Then the room went black and Darla came on the TV screen.

"Find me . . . find the truth, please help! Expose th—," she was cut off as the TV went blank again and the lights came back on.

"I think . . . I think that we have to get off Hawaii to solve this," Rick said.

"You aren't thinking," Ryu gulped.

"We're going to Bermuda." Rick's face was set and determined.

"Rick, that's dangerous. I mean . . ." Lexa said.

"We're Areos—nothing can kill us. Ryu'll be fine with us. But we are going to find the girl and we are going to uncover the truth and let these people cross over, even if we have to dive to the bottom of the ocean," Rick said to them.

"Rick . . . we can't . . . I mean are you sure?" Kari asked him, putting her hand on his shoulder.

"Kari, I'm sure. I'm completely sure that this is what we have to do, there's no other way,Kari. We have to find that suitcase," Rick said.

"Rick, she showed me things. There are images in my head. I know where to look . . . I can help," Kari said.

"No, Kari you and Lexa are going to stay here in Hawaii," Rick told her.

"Rick," Kari put her hand on his, "I'm not just your friend, I'm your best friend and friends stand by each other no matter what they go through. That's what we do," Kari told him as he looked up into her bright green eyes.

"Something . . . something might happen . . . I can't let you," Rick said.

Kari lifted his hand to her chest, pressing his palm to her heart. "Rick do you feel that? My heart beat? As long as that heart beats I will stand by your side because I'm your friend. I'm better—I'm a friend with benefits." The Areos searched his eyes for a response. His grey blue eyes were serious and tired while her brilliant grass green eyes were calm and caring. "As long as my heart beats," she said to him.

BERMUDA

It was two days later, the day before their trip to Bermuda. Kari was asleep on Rick's bed while Rick sat up on the computer. He was looking for data about the serum. Ryu and Lexa had gone to his house so Ryu was on his earpiece.

"Rick, why are we doing this again? I mean its nuts, isn't it?" Ryu asked him.

"Ryu, let me tell you something. Have you ever heard of the saying; 'it takes one to know one?'" Rick asked him and Ryu laughed softly.

"Well now, you two are up late again," Marshall floated into the room, upside down.

"Hello, Marshall, what are you doing?" Rick asked the spirit quietly.

"Does she know you're up?" Marshall asked pointing at the sleeping girl.

"No, Marshall is going to be quiet. Right?" Rick hissed.

"Yes, captain," Marshall said. The past few days Kari had been monitoring how much Rick slept, but this night he had gotten up on a hunch and called Ryu. He was still in his pajamas which consisted of boxers and a t-shirt. The fan swung lazily on the ceiling at three o'clock in the morning. They were going to be leaving for Bermuda in a while and would arrive there in 16 hours.

"Rick, this is crazy. There is no point in going through with this. I mean what is the girl's body going to help us with? Is she going to give us her pinky bone to wrap around the man who killed her?" Ryu asked sarcastically quoting a story from the book *Scary Stories* called 'The Haunt.'

"No I just think that's what she wants us to do. Maybe if we find her body it will tell us how she died and maybe we can explore the ship a bit and look in their cabin . . . you have the map right?" Rick asked.

"Yes, but I mean it's going to be hard to find, will we have enough air?" Ryu asked.

"You can grow gills—they are one benefit of being an Areos," Rick told him and Ryu laughed.

"All right, I guess you have this all figured out. Now, where are we staying?" Ryu asked.

"We're staying out on a yacht close to shore right near where the dog was seen on the suit case. Out a little ways from there is the boat," Rick replied.

"Rick, I hope you know what you're doing man." Said Ryu.

"I was just thinking the same thing," Rick said.

One sleepless night and one sleepless 6 hours later they were getting settled into the boat. Kari and Lexa were in one room and the Areos were in the other. It was getting dark and Kari wondered where Rick was. She walked to his and Ryu's room and looked in.

"Where's Rick, Ryu?" Kari asked him.

"How should I know? He's probably up top," he replied looking up from his computer.

"Thanks," Kari replied and walked up the stairs. She was wearing a pair of khaki capris again, this time with her black hoodie with 'Got Dance?' written on it. She heard the music from Final Fantasy 10 II. It was the prelude and it was on repeat. Her hair was up in a loose bun and she shivered as a strong wind blew then slowly died down. She walked up and smiled as she saw Rick sitting in a chair, watching the water below, the stereo on. She walked softly over to him and wrapped her arms around his neck.

"Rick?" she asked softly.

"What?" he replied looking up at her then looking back out to sea.

"Do you think that all this will turn out all right? I mean I'm scared that something might happen . . . there is so much we don't know," The Areos said, her soothing voice, calming Rick's own turmoil of thoughts.

"Kari I don't know . . . I just don't know. I mean there is Jackal's innocence and then there's Tarsal in the fire . . . the serum . . . then there's the girl herself. What could it be that made all this come to pass? What would drive a man so insane that he would kill his wife's daughter? Now that we know more, there is actually so much missing from the story," Rick said to her.

"Why are we pulled into this? Why did it have to be us?" Kari asked as she sat on the bench next to him. She looked out over the water, where he was looking.

"I don't know . . . I just don't know," Rick replied and looked over at her. She slowly turned her head to look back at him, her eyes locking into his. His hand was on hers, their fingers laced together. The beautiful deep black of the ocean water made the sky appear to never end. The deep dark blue of the sky filled with twinkling lights of the stars, the gentle rush of the waves on the shore added to the romantic feel of the moment as their lips met. All that could be heard was the gentle music and the rolling black waves but to them nothing more beautiful than that moment existed in the world. The full moon shone brightly, casting its brilliant silver light over the land like a fading spark of fire in a fireplace.

"They're so cute," Isabelle whispered to Marshall. He loved that boy like a son and Isabelle knew this.

"They're perfect for each other. Look at them Isabelle. It seems like nothing else exists, and nothing is going wrong. Makes you feel like everything is all right and they're not going to be making a dangerous trip to the bottom of the ocean. It makes my heart ache to see them, knowing that something will go wrong unfortunately for Rick. Whenever he gets something good in his life something else goes wrong." Marshall sighed watching the two teens. She was leaning back slightly, her fingers laced through the fingers on his other hand as well, which was on her waist.

"James, I hope they do come through. I don't mean to put them in any danger but I want my daughter and my love back, but there's something else at work here," she said to him.

"What? Tell me Isabelle—what's wrong?" the phantom asked.

"Jason . . . Marshall, it's Jason . . . he's the reason that everything is going wrong. He doesn't want anyone to know the truth because if they uncover the truth about him completely then his whole purpose will be in vain. He killed me and his cousin then he had his own brother hung, James. There is so much that I don't even know. But what I do know is that Jason will stop at nothing. He will do what he has to do," Isabelle said and the ghosts disappeared as the teens stopped.

"Did you hear that?" Kari asked.

"Hear what?" Rick asked, then he heard it to.

They looked out and there in the water was a ghost dog.

"It's the dog," Kari gasped as the apparition whined and barked then sank on top of the suitcase.

"Kari—it's trying to tell us something," Rick said.

"But what?" Kari's pupils shrunk so that she had none and she saw a memory that Darla had transferred. It was a memory of pure pain; she felt a sharp pain in her stomach and then felt herself being enclosed in a dark space then the memory ended and Kari was back on the ship lying on her back and Rick was leaning over her.

"What happened?" she asked sitting up.

"I . . . I don't know. You just suddenly grabbed at your stomach and collapsed," Rick said to her.

"It was a memory . . . a memory of something . . . it was strange," Kari said looking up at him. "I am going down there tomorrow and I am not coming back up until I find that suitcase," she told him and he nodded.

DROWNING

Rick woke to Kari gently shaking him, she was in her wet suit; on her wrist was the charm bracelet he had given her years before and on her right hand was the ring. He smiled sleepily.

"What's going on?" he asked.

"You and I are going down. Ryu and Lexa said that they were going to stay on the boat. I have water-proof earphones that automatically connect to them as we speak so we can communicate," she said handing him a black earpiece. He stood up and took the wet suit she handed him.

"It's wet," he laughed and she nodded as he slipped it on and she zipped it up.

"Rick . . . whatever happens . . ." She looked into those beautiful blue eyes again for what she feared might be the last time.

"Don't panic—we're going to be fine" he assured her as they walked up the stairs.

"Good morning, mates!" Ryu called to them.

"Morning Ryu, good morning, Lexa." Rick nodded to her.

"Good morning," Lexa said back. "Ready to go luggage hunting?" she asked and the two nodded while small slits appeared behind their ears—gills.

"Come on, we'll see you guys when we get back," Kari said. *If we get back,* she thought as they dove in.

"Let's look down there." She heard Rick's voice in her head. She followed as he swam down towards the white sands, beams of light created prisms of color as they swam. She looked around and her eyes opened wide as she saw the dog, the ghost dog with the white staring eyes was trying to dig. It looked up at her then disappeared.

"Rick over here," she said.

"I saw it," Rick replied. She swam over and they began to dig. The first thing they found made her scream under water, digging her nails into Rick's arm. It was the dog's skeleton. The salt in the water had bleached them to pure white and it looked so pathetic. She imagined Pooch like that and shivered. They dug further but didn't find anything. She snapped and the dog's bones disappeared to on board the ship and she heard Lexa scream and Ryu's laugh.

"What else?" Kari asked him.

"We wait for the dog," Rick replied and she nodded. They swam over to the wreckage.

"We're in," Kari said into the headpiece.

"Okay," Lexa's voice came over the mike.

"What room are we looking for?" Rick asked.

"You're looking for room 16A, a pretty fancy

room I'd say. It's on the top floor—turn to your left," Ryu replied.

"Rick something doesn't feel right here," Kari shivered looking over at him.

"I hear you . . . I know, it's too cold to—,' Rick stopped as they looked on and suddenly the entire ballroom was lit up and appeared as it did once long ago. Ghosts danced and then the whole room shook and a groan of the ship hitting something scared them all. There was the sound of a gunshot and Kari looked over at Rick.

"What was that? Was that a gunshot?" Kari asked him. Then suddenly her pupils disappeared again and she felt herself falling, sliding in a black hole. She tried to move but she was compressed. She heard a dog, barking and whining and she called out to it. Then she came to. She saw Rick's worried face and then Marshall and Isabelle's face behind him.

"Rick—Rick is she okay?" she heard Lexa's worried voice.

"I'm fine guys, just some cold chills," Kari laughed nervously.

"Okay, keep going then you're almost there," Ryu said to them.

"Well now, what are you two doing down here?" Isabelle asked as she and Marshall ballroom danced in the old broken room.

"We're trying to find your—," Kari saw the

dog and swam after it, her powerful legs propelling her forward.

"Where is she going?" Marshall asked and Rick sped past him to follow her. Isabelle and Marshall exchanged looks and floated after them.

"Here is their room—the dog is trying to get in," Kari said pointing to the room, while the dog was frantically scratching on the door. The dog turned towards Kari and instead of scratching again it waited for her to pet it. She changed her hand into a ghost hand and scratched the dog's ears.

"You miss your master. Don't worry, I'll reunite you with her," Kari said and the dog nodded and disappeared.

"Kari move," Rick said to her.

"What are you going to do?"

"I'm going to ram that door down."

"Rick, don't hit it too hard, the hinges are loose, it's just locked," Marshall told him.

"I know, Marshall," Rick replied then rammed his shoulder into the door knocking it in with a terrible wrenching sound.

"James," Isabelle cried and hung onto Marshall's other arm.

"Rick, look at it," Kari said slowly floating into the room. Along the ground heavy peeling scarlet blood stains could be seen. There was a large splatter of blood on one wall and then small handprints of blood on the floor, as if the person were trying to get away from something. Another line was strung across the floor then stopped and became a small puddle. More bloodstains were on the wall.

"James . . . Jason . . . he did all this . . ." the specter asked. Marshall nodded glumly. "James, my daughter . . . what pain she must have been in," Isabelle said and for the first time ghostly tears ran down the woman's face, coming to land on the colonel's jacket sleeve.

"Kari, what are you doing?" Rick asked as the girl knelt where the whole thing began.

"Look, she was shot here," Kari said and there was the noise of a gunshot and screaming then the groaning of the boat again. "Then he kicked her against the wall." There was a thud and a scream of pain and mixed shouts. 'Then she crawled along here." There was the sound of something hitting the floor then the sound of a body dragging on the ground, fingernails scratching on the wood floor. "Then she collapsed here." Kari said pointing to the blood puddle. There was the noise of groaning wood and ragged panted breathing along with small moans of pain. "Then he put her in the trunk," Kari said pointing to where a trunk would go. There were small puddles of dried blood and then they stopped and they heard echoing footsteps and a scream as the ship groaned again and the slamming of a wooden door and the locking of a latch.

"Kari, he killed her. Now all we have to do—," Rick stopped as out from under a bureau came the spirit of Darla Jackal. In her rather solid hand was a small pistol.

"Thank you, now please find my body . . . I must be laid to rest. Thank you . . . I will be with you soon, Mama," Darla said then faded away and the gun dropped to the ground. Rick picked it up as Isabelle cried again.

"Kari, don't you realize that we have more to do? We have to find Jason and Damien Jackal and we have to figure out what Jason did with the serum and what he was going to do with it," Rick said to her and Kari nodded.

"We need to find that trunk," she said and swam out to see the dog as it was running along in front of her, stopping every once in a while and turning, to see if she was still following.

"Kari, where are you going?" Ryu's voice came over the mike.

"To find that luggage," Kari replied. The dog stopped a few hundred feet away from her and began to try and dig, the same way it had with its body. "Ryu, try and examine those bones," Kari told him. She began to dig with the dog. After about 30 minutes her hand hit something hard. Rick, Isabelle and

Marshall finally caught up with her as she dug further.

"Kari . . . Kari slow down," Rick said to her and she stopped. He started to dig around the corner of the chest and slowly he exposed part of the case. He grabbed the strap and then felt Kari's hands next to his. They both pulled and the case suddenly came loose from the sand and they dragged it out.

Then Kari felt a shearing pain in her lungs as her gills disappeared and she was taking in water through her mouth but she wasn't breathing. She was sucking it in but it wasn't coming out through her gills. She closed her eyes as she tried to breath. Rick saw that she wasn't breathing, caught her hand and with a tug heaved the trunk into his hand. They broke the surface of the water but Kari still wasn't breathing. He panicked and swam frantically back to the boat. He threw the case over then passed Kari up to Ryu as his gills disappeared and he climbed back aboard. His legs were shaking, he was so terrified Kari was going to die. Water was slowly trickling from her mouth as her head flopped to the side.

"Come on Kari . . ." Rick said ripping the ear piece off and throwing it across the deck of the yacht.

Deep within Kari's mind she was in the suitcase, frantically screaming for help as it sunk to the bottom of the ocean, the water was slowly leaking in mixing with her own blood. She was drowning, she heard the dog above her, scratching and the sound of people screaming, the screams of the people on the ship that couldn't get off, the moans and shrieks of drowning people, people that were dying for no reason and the sad cries of men, women, and children . . . people she had known. She took in her last breath and breathed, "Mama,"—her limp lifeless body finally sinking to the bottom of the ocean, her faithful dog going with her, their stories forever forgotten.

"Kari, please . . . come on, you can't die on me here," Lexa said and the girl coughed, spraying water from her mouth, her body shuddered and she shook her head from side to side and then coughed up more water. Rick breathed a sigh of relief as Kari took his hand as her eyes opened and she pressed his palm against her heart.

"As long as this heart beats . . . ," she said and he pulled her into a strong embrace. She hugged him back, Darla was almost free.

Knowledge

They arrived back in Hawaii the next day with the trunk and a duffle bag with the dog's bones in it. Kari was still recovering from her brush with death, her legs still weak and the salt that had coated her lungs made it slightly hard for her to breathe but she was still as hearty as ever, she just needed to be monitored. They drove up in front of Rick's house and all their parents were there.

"Ryu, thank Ra." Ryu's mother, a mortal woman ran out, she embraced her son, kissing his face. His father walked out, he was tall and looked like a slightly older version of his son.

"We were so worried," Lexa's father ran out and embraced her in a hug. Rick's father and mother walked out and as his mother hugged him his father tousled his hair.

"We knew you could do it, son," Atem said proudly.

"Mum . . . Daddy!" Kari cried, tears pouring down her face as her parents embraced the weakened girl. "I was so scared I would never see you again, if it weren't for Rick I would still be down there." Kari's tears soaking her mother's shirt as she stroked her daughter's salty hair. Kari's father walked over to Rick, his mother let go of him and moved aside.

"Rick, thank you. You are brave . . . very brave," Kari's father said to the younger Areos shaking his hand.

"I was just helping a friend." Rick smiled as Kari grinned.

"I guess you're going to be helping that friend a lot more, eh?" Ryu laughed as his mother finally let go of him.

"I guess. Thank you sir, but I wasn't being brave," Rick said and Lexa scoffed.

"It was either bravery or pure stupidity," Lexa hugged her father one last time before he left.

"Thanks Lexa, I feel loved," Rick told her. Then they heard a gasp from Kari's mother.

"Your eyes, what happened to your eyes?" her mother asked looking into her eyes, the outside black ring was darker and the normally bright green of her eyes was now rimmed with deep brown. The black of her pupils was slightly foggy and misted.

"Nothing mum, I can still see fine, it's from the memories I guess—I'm okay," her daughter assured her.

"Are you going to be okay here?" her mother asked and Kari nodded as her parents got in the car.

"Don't worry. Naomi we'll take care of her," Atem said as they drove off.

"We'll see you when you get back, take care son," Ryu's father said as they walked back over to their house . . . right next door.

"I will Dad, don't worry," Ryu whispered.

"Now come on we need to find out what's in this trunk," Atem said lugging the heavy case out of the boot of Rick's car.

"All right," Rick replied and lifted his and Kari's suitcases out of the back as Ryu threw his and Lexa's over his shoulder.

"Let's see here," Atem said a little while later, examining the case with Marshall as the teens showered.

"It looks like a standard trunk used back then," Marshall said, floating upside down, cross legged with his arms folded across his chest.

"What did you find on the bones, James?" Atem asked as the ghost blinked and the bag opened revealing the dog's bones.

"They're untouched," Marshall replied as Pooch ran into the room, chased by Danny.

"Danny!" Atem laughed as the small sand fox jumped on top of the case, the puppy taking a running jump and landing with it then they raced back up through the house and Atem heard a laugh.

"Hey, Mr. D. What's up?" Tabby asked as she walked down the stairs. Tabby was wearing nothing, her fur covered her like a tight furry body suit so most of the time, unless they were going into a public place they never wore clothes. Her long tail swished back and forth as her long lion-like steely grey talons on her feet clicked on the hard cement floor of the basement, a part that was cut off from Rick's room, his father's research room. She tapped her steely gunmetal grey claws on the table as she walked over to him.

"Welcome, Tabitha, you are my scholar on bones and bodies . . . can you help your friends find out something information on metamorphs?" Atem asked and the humanoid nodded as Kari walked into the room, her long hair in a braid then wrapped up in a bun held up by chopsticks again. She was wearing an evergreen hoodie that read 'Angel Academy' in a circle around the star of David. On a patch on her right sleeve was the number 1223, signifying the class number she was in. Rick, Lexa, Ryu and Tabby all had one. Humanoids went there too because they possessed powers like the Areos. She was wearing a pair of loose black carpenter capris. She laughed as she saw the strange set of people before her, a seemingly normal man who was actually one of the most powerful Seraphim in all of Heaven, a phantom floating upside down and cross legged and a humanoid, her tail twitching impatiently, her ears cocked forward.

"Well, now are you a mixture?" she laughed as she walked forward.

"You smell like death," the humanoid said sniffing Kari, "Why, I thought Areos couldn't die."

"I didn't die but I almost did." It was then that they all noticed a large old leather bound book full of marks and tassels. It was locked and on top of it was her computer. She set it down, opened her computer and waved her hand over the lock and it snapped open. The young Areos flipped through the pages and stopped on a certain page.

"Do you know what this is?" she asked and Atem walked over to her.

"It's your book, the book of the Angels . . . but how . . . ?" Atem asked.

"It's mine, all of us get a copy but mine was passed on to me by my grandmother." Kari replied. She noticed a strong resemblance between Rick and his father. They both had the same spiky brown hair and blue eyes but his father was slightly more built, his shoulders were broader and his chest was wider. They had almost the same personality, caring and kind but serious and reserved at the same time.

"You and Rick are a lot alike, you know that?" Kari said.

"His mother tells me that all the time, I thought it was just her." Atem smiled.

"No, you two are, she's right . . . you both love

to help people and you both care deeply in a way most people are afraid to care, with all of their souls and hearts. You are not afraid to love," Kari told him. She looked at the picture in her book, it was a picture of what the serum could do to people that used it for the wrong reasons.

"I know now why they call you the Angel of Serenity and Wisdom, you know things that many people your age do not," Atem replied and she shook her head.

"Knowledge does not make a person but knowledge can break one," she replied softly pointing at the computer screen. "Jason Jackal knew that the serum could be used to change one person into another but what he *didn't* know that Darrel Tarsal *did,* was that the serum would turn into the most powerful poison known to man and angel alike if used for what the producer believed to be the wrong reason. That is, *if* they succeeded in getting it out of them. Darla knew that her power could be used for good so she willingly gave serum to Tarsal but when she wouldn't give it to Jason he killed her but, what does all this have to do with Damien?" Kari told them. Rick and the others had walked into the room during her explanation and were now standing behind the Tabitha and Rick's father.

"We still have work to do," Lexa said. In her hands was her laptop and earpiece. She walked over to Kari and sat down. "We are going to work until we can't keep our eyes open at all," Lexa looked over at Kari.

"I better go buy out Starbucks," Atem said.

"Go ahead, we have a long couple of days ahead of us," Ryu replied and Atem walked back up the stairs.

"All right, Tabby—you work on checking out the dog's bones and try and see if there is anything different about them and Marshall, you help her. Rick, Ryu—you two start trying to open that trunk and don't break it, there might be more to it than it seems and Lexa and I will do some more research on Damien Jackal—maybe he had a bigger part in this than we originally thought," Said Kari.

THE TRUNK

It was one in morning and they were still working on it. They boys were examining the trunk, still trying to figure out how to open it. The lock was securely fastened in place and the hinges were still firm and untouched. They weren't allowed to break it open so they had to figure it out.

"Hey look at this!" Tabby said and Kari looked up.

"What is it?" she asked and the tabby held up a vial.

"What in the world is that?" Rick asked.

"We found it, *inside* one of the dog's leg bones," the cat said.

"Inside? Let me see that," Kari asked and Tabby handed her the vial and continued to work with Marshall.

"There's something inside it," Lexa said and Kari opened the cork on top. She shook the small vial and a piece of rolled paper fell out.

"What is this?" Kari asked opening it.

"An SOS? I don't know," Ryu replied.

"Well, how did the dog get it *inside* one of its *bones*?" Lexa asked.

"Darla . . . she could have put it in there, her

spirit could have while they were falling to the bottom of the ocean," Kari said. She was looking at it. It looked like it was backwards.

"Let me see that," Rick said taking the paper from her. He looked at it. "It's . . . backwards or something. And it's blurry," he said as Marshall looked at it, too.

"Perfect time for a mirror," he whispered.

"Marshall, thank you," he said and ran into the bathroom. Kari and the others followed him. " *'Finders of this note, a great evil will oppose you . . . I am sorry for pulling you into this for if you found this dog you will have found my body . . . I am sure that you are wonderful creatures and I am pleased you are helping me but please be careful, this evil will turn one of you against the others and you must fight each other to save those whom this man has already destroyed. Please, I am begging you, take great caution . . . '* " Rick read.

"She knows something's going to happen," Tabby said.

"Yeah, but which one of us?" Lexa asked and all eyes were on Kari.

"We'll just have to wait and see," Kari said weakly.

"I don't want to do this anymore," Lexa broke down, falling to her knees, tears pouring from her eyes as she raised her face to the heavens, "I don't want anyone to be turned against us . . . I don't want this to be a part of my life anymore . . . it's causing me too much pain," the angel cried to the ceiling.

"I know Lexa, I know but we can't back down now," Kari said dropping down next to her friend.

"You're right, but we should have never gotten into this in the first place. I mean we should have left well enough alone. I mean you've come so close to dying, and we're doing all this crazy stuff for what? For nothing," the girl cried.

"Lexa, listen to me. Calm down. We're all going to be okay and if we didn't have a reason we wouldn't do it but . . ." Kari sat in front of her friend, taking her hands in hers. "We do. . . . how would you feel if you were killed and couldn't return to your mother? What if no one helped you because it was getting rough or because they didn't think it was safe? Just because life gets a little rocky every once in a while doesn't mean you just give up, you have to persevere and if you make a mistake don't dwell on it, learn from it and keep going because somewhere . . . somewhere there's got to be some good . . . if you hit a road block go around it. Don't you see, we're all in this together and we're not going to back down because if we do then we have failed—we have failed Darla and her mother, we have failed Jackal, we have failed the people that believe we can do this and are rooting for us along the way. Lexa, we are a team and we stick together no matter what. As long as this heart beats I will be there for you and we all will be there for each other," Kari said to Lexa and she stopped crying at the sound of her best friend's voice—there was something different about her at that moment. It was then that Lexa realized that she wasn't just her best friend. Kari was a powerful being, older than she was and wise beyond her years.

"Kari . . . I . . . thank you," she said and the girl hugged her tightly.

"We will always be here for you, no matter what," Rick smiled and Ryu nodded.

"We all will," Tabby said.

"Forever, no matter what happens—we will all be there for each other," Marshall added in.

"Remember 'The Three Musketeers'? Remember their motto and ours?"

"All for one and one for all," they all said together.

"Now, let's get back to work and help Darla and her mother," Kari said helping her friend to her feet.

"Yeah, we can do this," Ryu said.

A few hours later they were working and Kari suddenly had a break through.

"Lexa, look at this," Kari said tapping her fingernail on the screen. "Damien Jackal graduated top of his class. He was a research scientist of his time," Kari smiled.

"Kari, are you thinking what I'm thinking?" Lexa asked.

"Damien and Darrel were working together on cultivating the serum into a medication to heal people and help those who lost limbs. They were research-ing mutations . . . and Darla was helping," Kari said and Lexa nodded as there was a snap from behind them and the wooden box creaked open. Rick gasped and Ryu's eyes grew wide.

"Ka-Kari come here," Tabby shivered and Kari walked over to look in the box and screamed. Inside was the body of Darla Jackal but she wasn't destroyed, her body was perfectly preserved. Her stomach was stained a deep soggy crimson color and there was the hole from the gunshot wound. Pooch jumped up on the table and sniffed. Her long brown hair was draped over her small shoulders and her eyes were closed, her pale lips were open as if she had just taken in a breath.

"Darla . . . Darla, I'm so sorry. I wish you wouldn't have had to die like this," Kari said softly and Darla's ghost appeared in the room.

"*Thank you. Thank you so much . . .*" Darla said. "*I am now able to cross over . . . and I have, but my father . . . what about him?*" she asked and Isa-belle appeared. The mother and daughter embraced each other ghostly grey tears pouring down their faces.

"We'll help him as well," Kari nodded.

"Thank you," Isabelle breathed, stroking her daughter's hair. "Thank you."

Damien Jackal's Research

Six o'clock at night . . . Rick looked up at the clock. Isabelle and Darla were sitting in a corner of the room talking quietly while Rick and Ryu carefully lifted the girl's body out of the trunk.

"Why would anyone do this?" Ryu asked looking at the hole in the 5 year-old's stomach.

"I don't know," Rick replied as they gently lifted her into a coffin. They were sending her to her relatives who had heard what they had done and Isabelle's granddaughter was crying and telling her relatives, as Rick had called to tell them, that they were sending her to be buried with her mother. Isabelle had another child, a son who had been sixteen at the time of the fire and now he was an old man, but still remembered his mother. He thanked them for bringing his sister back to them and apparently he had passed earlier that day. The young man's spirit was now with his mother and little sister. He was a handsome young man with brown hair pulled back in a ponytail and a yellow vest. His face was neat and clean shaven.

"So, you are the kids who helped my little sister?" he asked floating over.

"Yeah, what's your name?" Kari asked him.

"Me? I'm Derek. My father named me," Derek said.

"Who was your father?" Lexa asked looking over.

"Damien Jackal," Derek replied coolly.

"Hmmm . . . quite a conspiracy here, eh Isabelle?" Marshall laughed.

"I loved Damien Jackal. He was a great man with a noble cause . . . he would have been awarded the Nobel Prize for his work." She smiled.

"Ah, understand now, but Isabelle did you know anything about their work?" Kari asked and she shook her head.

"I'm sorry no I didn't," Isabelle said.

"I did, my father was training me to be like him. Oh, I would spend hours with him and Uncle Darrel; we had so much fun," the young man said looking off into the distance.

"Can you tell us about it?" Kari asked turning to him, her computer in her lap.

"Well, isn't that a bright little thing," Derek said looking at the computer. "And why are you wearing men's clothes." The entire room let out a groan except for Isabelle. Darla laughed.

"Please don't ask. I've been asked that too many times," Kari said to him. "But can you tell me something about Damien, please?" Kari asked and he nodded. The young man sat on the desk as best he could, looking like he was sitting but he was actually floating.

"Well, my father and Darrel worked underground in a blocked-off part of the old rail station, remember that place, Ma?" he asked and she nodded. "It had a large basement and no one ever went down there, they still don't. It's still there to this day. But we would go down there and Darla would come sometimes and they would always take some serum. They collected it just before they started each day. For shape shifters or metamorphs like Darla, they could change and stay that way as long as they wanted, then change back, but for humans it was different. They could change with the serum but then they would stay that way until they took more and changed back but there were lasting side effects such as scars on the other person's body could be transferred to the others. We tried this many times on rats and other animals but then one day a boy stumbled into our lab. He was maybe 14 and his right leg was missing, so we decided to ask him if he wanted our help and he said sure but then we asked him for a favor. We asked him if he would let us try the reversal serum on him—we had an antidote for the serum in case he didn't like it that could reverse the process—a serum we knew worked. So he took it and before our eyes his leg rebuilt itself. He looked at it then stood up and ran around crying tears of joy. It was then we realized our mistake. For on his leg was a large black scar. Instead of completely healing it he had gotten his leg back from before it was amputated but the good thing was that instead of it having to be amputated it had healed and instead had created this black scar." Derek said while Kari typed it all down.

"Then what happened? I mean is there more to your research . . . did you do anymore human testing?" Kari asked and Derek nodded.

"When we had perfected it, the man thanked us and had run out and we smiled at his happiness. It was then we realized something else, the serum could be used to get rid of scars and we could even develop it to heal diseases such as the black plague because we could restore victims back to the way they were. So we started right away and Darla was there the entire rest of the time," Derek said as his little sister sat in his lap.

"They were so funny always tickling me to get me to give them serum." Darla laughed and Kari looked at her.

"They tickled you to get the serum?"

"Yeah, each metamorph had a certain way of releasing the serum and Darla's way was to tickle her, and she is ticklish. We would tickle her and make her laugh and her body would release the serum," Derek smiled squeezing his sister's sides and she giggled.

"Where did the serum come from?" Kari asked

and Derek smiled again turning his sister over. On her back, just below her neck, between her shoulder blades was a small black circle. A drop of ghost serum dropped from it as he tickled her again.

"Derek! St-stop!" the girl giggled as he set her back up again.

"Wow, that's pretty cool." Lexa smiled at the giggling girl.

"Go on what else happened?" Kari asked.

"Well, after they would tickle me they would set me down and for some reason they'd make me take these funny tests, they would take my heart rate and examine my blood and all kinds of things. Then on my 3rd birthday my daddy gave me my Lassie," the little girl said and out of nowhere the dog jumped into the room. Its eyes were brown instead of dead white and in its mouth was a rag doll. Darla took the doll from the collie dog and hugged it, turning back to the others. The collie sat down next to Derek, under the table.

"Sometimes they'd even make me change into something else and examine me," the little girl smiled.

"We did that because we wanted to see if her scars and other things carried over and unfortunately they did. We finally started to develop the disease serum and Darla was especially interested because her friend . . . who was it Darla, Sara?"

"No silly, Mary Lou," Darla shook her head. "Mary Lou died from the cancer . . . she was my best friend. I wanted to help people . . . I did . . ." Darla smiled.

"Yes, well she wanted to help others like her friend and create the medical serum so she began to get us supplies by buying things we needed by changing into one of us so we could continue working and go and get whatever we needed," Derek said.

"Then he came . . . he came down and hurt Daddy," Darla whispered darkly.

"Then one night Jason came down while we were working and tried to kill my father but it didn't work because before he could bleed to death we used the serum. We hadn't started testing so we didn't know what was going to happen but his wounds healed and—"

There was a loud snap and the sound of screeching boards. They all turned around to see Ryu and Rick peering into the bottom of the trunk, boards were all over the floor and a crowbar was in Rick's hand, he looked very pleased with himself.

"What was that about?" Kari asked walking over.

"This." Rick lifted a large airtight metal bow out of the bottom of the trunk. Then something caught her eye on the trunk's side.

"Look at this." She looked for something in the

room and saw what she was looking for, paint thinner.

"Are you trying to get high?" Rick asked and instead she walked over, put some of the thinner on a paper towel.

"Property of . . . DAMIEN JACKAL! I was right!" Kari exclaimed. Derek and Darla rose and walked over. "Tabby, come here and open this box."

Tabitha walked over and looked at it then with one swipe sliced the metal lid off.

"That's my father's hand writing, he always wrote in short hand," Derek said.

"Derek, are you saying that this is all your father's?" Kari asked pulling out a grimy notebook. But neat underneath all the papers and folders and notebooks was a letter in an ivory envelope. It was addressed 'To whom it may Concern':

" 'To Whom It May Concern:

I am writing this letter under my own will and of completely sound mind. You have found it—the thing I strived to create. After years and months of working in a dark dank laboratory with my son, daughter, and cousin we have finally created three different medications. Inside a small padded box within this one you will find six vials.

Kari stopped reading and pulled out the small box and opened it. Inside were six bottles like he had said.

"'The first three of these are the actual medications. They are labeled according to their purpose, I pray that someone will find this and complete what I began, although I have small hope that this chest will ever be found. Inside this box is all of my research and notes. As I said I am of sound mind and in the purest of calms but something is looming in my future. I know it because my brother will soon have me killed, for what I will not know until it comes, but I thank you and pray that you will please finish what I started. Damien Jackal.' " Kari finished and looked up.

"Jackal knew something was going to happen—he knew," Ryu gasped.

"He was brilliant. Look at this," Tabby said lifting one of the vials up gingerly in her padded fingers. "They are labeled and the ingredients are on them . . ." The humanoid looked over.

"This keeps getting more confusing and more confusing," Kari sighed.

Jason Jackal's Plan

"This is so extensive," Atem said; his son had called him down a few hours earlier and shown him the research. "He has everything—from Darla's test results to the exact small details of each experiment. He was an amazingly brilliant man," Atem said looking at the pages.

"One thing. What was Jason going to do with the serum? I mean we have our speculations, but we don't quite know yet," Kari said.

"I know. We have to keep looking—something will come up," Ryu said and Lexa nodded at her friend.

"All right, but I think we're going to have to turn to someone I know none of us are going to like; we're going to have to call Kioko," Kari said. The whole room let out a groan in unison. Kioko was Rick's aunt. She was half cat and half Areos but she was the most intelligent scientist that anyone could think of. She had a plain personality, she was very drab and liked to keep to herself.

"Well, while you're at it, why don't you just get my whole family in on it why don't you?" Rick grumbled. His grandfather was Ra himself and he and Atem got along, like . . . well, like opposite ends of a magnet.

"Come on, we need her Rick. I know no one likes her but she's the best scientist we have and maybe—well, she's always complaining about not having anything interesting to do. Maybe we could ask her to finish Damien's work," Kari said putting hands on Rick's knees.

"Kari, do you know how much of a pain she is though? I mean Dad doesn't even like her and she's his sister," Rick said.

"Please Rick, none of us like her but she can help us," Kari said.

"Well, all right but I mean I hope you're right," Rick replied, keeping his eyes on her hand.

"I knew you would understand," Kari smiled and walked back over to her seat. The entire room had just watched this exchange and then just turned away as if they hadn't as Rick looked around at them. He picked up his earpiece and called his aunt.

"Kari, what was that? Jeez, talk about breaking the monotony with some feminine appeal . . . I mean how do you do it?" Lexa asked her and Kari laughed softly.

"There is a tremendous power that comes along with being female," Kari said softly.

"How do you do it? I admit you are the master," Lexa inquired darkly, a mischievous look on her face.

"Hmmm . . . Master? I don't know about that, but, what can I say—I enjoy being a girl," Kari giggled softly then they both looked up as a grumpy Rick walked over and tossed her his earpiece.

"She wants to talk to you," he said looking at her, a slightly pained look in his eye then walked back to his father and Ryu.

"He-hello?" Kari asked putting on the earphone.

"Is this Kari?" Kari heard Kioko's voice on the other line but it almost wasn't her voice.

"Ye-yes ma'am it is," Kari replied and threw Rick a look across the room and he shrugged.

"I'm coming but I need to ask you a question—how many vials does he have? I've been looking information up on his research and it says that he was just working on one," Kioko said.

"But the information wasn't released . . ." Kari said softly, sensing something strange was going on here.

"Well, it's on here and it says that he was trying to discover a way to destroy things, but that's not what the serum was used for . . . by the metamorphs . . . I mean . . ."

"That's not the right information. Hurry and come over; we have the right stuff, hurry please,"

Kari said and Kioko said she would be there in a few minutes and hung up.

"Here, she sounds happy she has something to do . . . she's coming over in a few minutes," Kari told them and threw the earpiece to Rick.

"All right, good. I think that this serum might give us a whole new Kioko—I hope." Atem had a slightly sarcastic unsure look on his face.

"How do you do it?" Lexa asked again as Kari turned back to her computer.

"Like I said, I give people what they want and they give me what I want but to tell you the truth, Kioko sounded anxious to be involved," Kari told her and then turned back to her computer.

"So, what are we looking for again?" Lexa asked.

"What was Jason's purpose? What was his use for the serum?" Kari asked and looked at the clock. "Oops! I'll be back in about an hour—see you then," Kari smiled then ran out.

"Where's she going?" Rick asked and Lexa shrugged.

"I don't know. Why are you asking me?" Lexa shook her head.

"She's going down to get her hair cut," Tabby said not looking up from the trunk, she was examining.

"She's what?" Rick asked making a move to go after her but the Tabitha's tail stopped him.

"She's not getting it cut very short. She just says that it's a bother and that she's going to cut it; you have no say in it," the humanoid pushed him back down, still not looking up.

"Oh, you should see her hair short, Rick. It's so pretty, it turns into waves around her shoulders." Lexa sighed. "I want her hair," she said then turned back to the computer.

"Lexa, wasn't Kari looking for Jason's reason for wanting the serum?" Atem asked and Lexa nodded.

"Why?" she walked over.

"Too late—she left, because Damien knew," Atem said interestedly.

"He knew why Jason wanted the serum?" Lexa asked him and he nodded.

"One mystery ends and another starts," Ryu said pessimistically.

"Stop being a pessimist Ryu." Rick said to the smaller boy.

"Okay but it's true," Ryu sighed.

"Jason was going to use the serum to create a changing medicine, or something that would change a soldier into an enemy soldier or lieutenant or something of that sort. Then he was going to sell it to the government and make money off of Darla by selling her to the government." They all heard Damien Jackal's voice from the TV.

"Damien—Damien—you're alright!" Isabelle ran over.

"Isabelle, I don't have much time. Please you need to hurry. Please figure out how to destroy this man. He's trying to use what's left of my serum to create a body for himself—hurr-" Damien's face disappeared.

"He's trying to create a serum to give himself his body back? Where's Kari when you need her?" Lexa sighed then the door opened and Kioko walked down. She had light tan fur all over. Her tan ears poked out the top of her brown hair. But her face wasn't cinched like Tabby's it was a normal human face and her feet didn't have talons.

"Where's the serum?" she asked them.

"Over here, Kioko. I'll show you," Atem said and led her across the room.

THE ANTI-SERUM

A few hours later it was four o'clock in the morning, July 3rd. Kari had come in earlier, her hair cut around her shoulders, wavy and still deep brown.

"How are you doing?" she asked Rick. Atem had fallen asleep with his head on the papers. Kioko was nodding off on her hand which was holding up her head and Ryu was sound asleep with Lexa's head on his chest and his arm around her shoulders. They were the only two awake; even Tabby was curled up in a ball in the corner.

"Not perfect—you?" he asked brushing a piece of hair out of her face.

"To tell you the truth I've been better," she replied. "Rick, what do we do whenever Jason comes? I mean, what if he's found a way to control one of us? Maybe that's what Darla meant when she said he will turn one of us against the other?" she asked reaching down to pet Pooch.

"Kari, I don't know, I really don't. I mean it could be any of us," Rick sighed shaking his head.

"Jason has power beyond us; none of our attacks can hurt him."

"But he's going to be either possessing one

of us or another's body. All we have to do is banish him," Rick told her, cupping her chin in his hand.

"That might be hard. We don't know what he can do—we don't know what we're up against," she whispered.

"What was it you said? Ah yes—'if the road gets rocky there must be a smooth place somewhere,'" Rick replied quietly, his voice slightly gravelly, the sound of a boy's voice just deepened into manhood.

"Rick . . . Rick we can't just . . . I mean . . . this is like driving a car blindfolded," she said, her hands on his knees again.

"Hmmm . . . I could do that . . . if you wanted me to, then again it's a little dangerous to try and drive without being able to see," Rick whispered as their lips met, this rare elation a welcome embrace. He was getting that feeling again, his thoughts began to go hazy.

"I'm not completely asleep yet," Atem said clearing his throat at them and they pulled back away from each other. Rick glared at his father sourly. Atem just smiled.

"Thanks Dad . . ." Rick said sarcastically.

"Well now, that was an awkward situation," Kari laughed nervously.

"Sorry, I couldn't help it," Atem chuckled.

"Not funny," Rick hissed. He was grumpy now; nothing wanted him to kiss his girlfriend—not her brain, not the ghost dog, and now not his father—the whole world was turning against him.

"Oooohh, it's okay, there's more where that came from," Marshall chortled.

"Shut it, James," Rick grouched. Kari patted his knee.

"Stop. Just let it go, okay?" she raised her eyebrows, her face looking like she was about to laugh.

"The world hates me," Rick groaned.

"Oh, stop being such a drama queen," Marshall told him and that made both Atem and Kari laugh hysterically.

"James," Isabelle's voice came from the corner.

"Yes, *mother*," Marshall replied sarcastically.

"What's all the noise?" Lexa asked, opening her eyes. She saw Rick being grumpy, Kari laughing with his father and Kari's hands on Rick's knees. "Yet another interrupted kiss, Rick?" Lexa laughed.

"N-no! Mar-Marshall jus-just called R-Rick a Dra-drama Q-Queen!" Kari laughed; tears were forming in her eyes.

"Oh, now that's funny," Ryu laughed with Lexa.

"Are you laughing at me?" Rick asked playfully.

"Maybe . . . why?" she asked back.

"Because, I don't like being laughed at." Rick laughed finally then Kioko's head shot up.

"I'VE REMEMBERED THE ANTI-SERUM!" Kioko cried out and rushed over to a bag that she carried everywhere.

"The anti-serum for what?" Tabby asked, waking up.

"The anti-serum for the medicine that Jason is trying to make. Here Kari, if he had succeeded just throw that on him but if not then you're stuck," Kioko threw the vial to her. Kari put it in a small crystal around her neck.

"Thanks, Kioko," Kari said and Kioko nodded.

"Now, I'm going back to bed," Kioko said and walked up the stairs. Kari laughed.

"Now that every one's awake what are we going to do?" Lexa asked.

"Go back to bed?" Ryu suggested sleepily.

"No, we're going to keep working. Now all we need to do is piece together all the parts of this crazy mixed up story and I know the perfect place to start," Kari said turning to her computer. She began to type and Rick watched over her shoulder.

"Listen to this . . . there's one more thing . . ." Atem said to them.

"What is it, Mr. Daniels?" Kari asked.

"Jason Jackal was . . ." Atem stopped as his eyes opened wide.

"Jason Jackal was what?" Kari asked.

"Jason Jackal was put in a mental institution at an early age for saying that he wasn't able to—"

"I wouldn't finish that sentence if I were you."

They all heard a voice from behind them. Kari swung around.

"You," she whispered before everything went black.

THEIR CAPTURE

Kari woke up feeling very up in the air. Literally. She was hanging with her wrists above her head chained to the wall. She was wearing a white dress, the sleeves were down to her elbows and she guessed that usually the dress would have reached just below her knee. It was kind of like a t-shirt without the tight neck hole because the top of it was square cut so that it slightly showed her shoulders. She looked around and saw that the others were there. Rick was hanging with his chin to his chest, around his waist was a kilt that was uneven and tatty. She looked across from her and there was Ryu, in the same kilt as Rick. She looked directly to her left and she saw Tabby, she wasn't wearing anything as usual. Her fur looked unclean and unwashed though. She looked over again and saw that Lexa was there in the same dress but Atem wasn't. Atem wasn't there. *Maybe he just didn't get through . . . I mean . . . maybe the ghost didn't take him*, she thought worriedly.

"Kari . . . Kari where are we?" she heard Lexa's voice; it was weak as though she couldn't breath.

"I-I don't know," Kari replied listening to her voice echo throughout the well-like room. It seemed as though they were hanging in a dungeon but there wasn't a floor underneath them. It was just a huge black hole.

"Oh, so you're awake,"

Kari heard a pebble fall off some place hit a wall then it fell, straight down but didn't make a sound after that.

"Who is this?" she asked looking around.

"You know who this is." She heard the man's voice again. She just couldn't place it, it was sort of high pitched and nasally, that kind of voice that everyone hates listening to—you know the kind your math teacher gets when they have a cold? Yeah that kind of sound.

"No, no as a matter of fact I don't," Kari sassed back. She knew who it was but she didn't want to.

"Well, now—a fiery one eh?"

She watched in horror as Jason Jackal floated down to face her.

"Where . . . where's Atem?" she growled at him. Lexa apparently was being completely silent.

"Don't you worry about him . . . don't you worry . . . he's fine, he was just having a little chat with me."

"Leave him alone. He's a better man then you will ever be," she spat in his face.

"Why you little . . ."

Her eyes opened wide as the man back handed her, slamming the side of her head against the wall, a cut now on the side of her head dripping a small amount of blood.

"Try me. I won't break . . ." Kari spat in his face again. This time he didn't hesitate and he slapped her, a small amount of blood now dripping from her bottom lip.

"You little worm . . . how could you even dream of trying to take me down?" Jason asked her.

"Because I'm going to," she back sassed.

"What? Did you want to say that to me again?" the man asked coming in close to the angel's face.

"Leave her alone!" Kari heard Lexa's voice. The man floated over looking upset.

"Oh, look how cute, the girl scouts are standing up for each other." He laughed maliciously. *"Even better—you can all die together then. And don't say you can't die girl, because if I can die you can,"* the man spat at Kari.

"Now come on, mister. Can't we settle this like normal non-mentally incapacitated people?" Kari asked and before she could say any more the man had taken her jaw in his powerful hand.

"What did you say?" the infuriated man hissed at her, squeezing her jaw until she thought it would break.

"I said—that you are a mental—a nut case—a mentally incapacitated individual," she hissed back and he again slammed her head into the wall except this time her eyes glowed blue and she didn't hit it, he hit the wall opposite of her. He slammed into the wall with such force that the wall cracked and an indention was left where he had been.

"Yeah! Go Kari . . . it's your birthday, go Kari it's your birthday!" Lexa sang.

"Care to try that again?" Jason asked her, then waved his hand and ropes appeared out of nowhere and began to bind her body tightly.

"Stop—stop it! You're an evil man—stop!" Lexa yelled at him, tears pouring down her face, Kari's body now hung limply on the wall.

"Why would you even want to hurt something as beautiful as an angel?" Tabby cried after Lexa spoke.

"What is beauty if it isn't useful?" Jason replied evilly. *"But okay, I hope you'll hang around."* He laughed wickedly at his own sick joke then floated back up and out of sight.

"Kari!" Lexa cried to her friend who wasn't moving.

"I'm here," she coughed, her head throbbing painfully.

"That was a really weird dream—," Ryu grumbled and then opened his eyes to see that it wasn't a dream. "Holy cow!"

"All right, where are we?" Ryu asked.

"We don't know. All we know is that Rick's

out cold and we can't find his dad and Jason has his body back," Lexa said.

"RICK!" Ryu bellowed across the room and Rick jolted up.

"Wow, we should have you around more often," Kari laughed as Rick looked around wildly.

"Where-"

"WE DON'T KNOW!" they all yelled at him and he looked blown away.

"Okay, there goes that question . . . uh . . . Ryu did your head get really big and slam into the wall while you were sleeping because it sure does look like it," Rick asked.

"What a time for jokes," Kari laughed with Tabby and Lexa.

"No, huh what in the . . . ?" Ryu looked up and saw the indent in the wall.

"Kari blasted Jason into the wall," Lexa said and looked over. Kari's jaw was beginning to bruise and her lip was swelling.

"You look like you got into a fight with the wall and the wall won," Ryu laughed and then slammed into the wall behind him. "YOWCH!" Ryu cried.

"Cool it, Kari, he's our friend," Lexa hissed at her. Kari's eyes stopped glowing and she apologized.

"I'm sorry I just hate that man. He hit me—

I'm going to kill him if it takes every drop of my power."

"That might be overkill isn't it?" Rick asked.

"Overkill is better than under kill isn't it?" Kari replied.

"Whatever," Tabby said.

ATEM'S FINAL REVELATION

"How long do you think we've been hanging here?" Lexa asked. They had no concept of time there.

"Must be a good few days," Ryu sighed. "We missed the 4th of July."

"You're worried about the 4th of July and we're hanging on a wall like ham? What goes on in your head?" Kari asked him.

"Have we figured a way out of here yet?" Rick asked then out of nowhere Marshall appeared in the middle of them.

"Marshall!" they all said together.

"Hello. Look I don't have much time. Here." He handed a small key to Kari. "Hurry up, drop down, it's an illusion, the bottom is just a few feet below you—hurry," the ghost whispered and then disappeared in a puff of smoke. Kari reached over and unlocked her chains then floated over to Lexa and unlocked hers and she dropped down. She unlocked Rick's, her eyes locking into his for a moment before he dropped and she moved to the others. She dropped down with them, the key around her neck.

"Where's my dad?" Rick asked; he had forgotten about him until just then.

"Rick, we don't know, but we need to get out of here. Come on," Kari said and began to walk up a set of stairs.

"Kari, how do you know this is the way?" Lexa asked a few minutes later to break the silence.

"I don't, but it's the *only* way so therefore it must be the way," Kari replied.

"Kari, if the floor was just an illusion maybe we're all just in an illusion," Ryu suggested and a stone from the steps fell down into the abyss beneath them.

"Did that seem like an illusion?" Kari asked and he shook his head.

"No, that was very real," he replied and kept walking. They came up in the middle of an old stone hallway.

"Kari . . . Kari, this looks awfully familiar," Tabby squeaked, her tail puffed out like a pipe cleaner.

"Shhhh . . . hush, don't say a word," Kari whispered so quietly that the others had to strain to hear. "And don't move a muscle." She almost silently hissed through her teeth.

Down the hallway came the exact person they didn't want to see. Jason Jackal was walking down the hallway, his sullen face split in a grin.

"Time to hurt someone . . ." he sang and walked into a room then came back out a dagger in his hand.

"No, not yet . . . don't worry, you're time will come," he said into the room then turned to walk back down the hallway.

"Dad," Rick hissed.

"No, Rick calm down . . . just stay here, we'll go in a second." She watched as Jason turned into another room.

"Come on," she whispered and they walked into the room where Jason had just been. There on the wall was Rick's father, hanging, his wrists tied together by a rope hung from the ceiling. He was bruised and there were cuts and scratches all across his body. His powerful shoulders slumped as they cut him down. He was barely breathing and his heart beat was irregular.

"Gotcha!" Kari felt arms around her, squeezing her against a powerful body.

"Let her go!" Rick stood up.

"You want to save your girlfriend? Well you can't. You take your father and I'll take the girl—thanks," Jason growled evilly. "We're even," he said then disappeared.

"Ryu," Lexa cried and hugged him. "She's gone, he took her—he took Kari!" she cried.

"I know—I know, Lexa," Ryu said, "but this is no time to panic."

"I know what Kari would say at a time like this," Tabby said. " 'All for one and one for all'—we swore—'as long as this heart beats I will stand by your side.'" Tabby traced a circle on the floor with one of her long talons.

"You're right. 'As long as our hearts beat we will be there for each other,'" Rick said, and for the first time in four years of his life he cried, tears poured from his eyes, running down his face as he slammed his fist into the wall angrily.

"Rick . . . stop . . . ," Tabby said. "Fighting hate with hate only creates more hate." The cat said putting her padded hand on his shoulder. "She would kill you if she saw you like this," Tabby said and wiped his tears away with one of her paws.

"Tabby . . . I just . . . I mean. . . ." He felt Ryu's hand on his shoulder.

"We understand—we all cared for her—we all did, but she's not dead, we're going to get her back, just wait and see," Ryu said and they heard a groan from Atem.

"Dad!" Rick knelt down by his father's side.

"Rick . . . hey . . . listen . . . to the end of what I was going to say. Jason Jackal was put in an insane asylum at an early age because he claimed that he couldn't die and was found about to shoot himself to prove it . . . ," Atem said.

"But he died . . . which meant . . ."

"That he could die—but there's something about Kari—he wants it . . . ," Atem coughed.

"Oh yeah, I remember now. She said something about a fountain of youth or something," Lexa said and Ryu nodded.

"No, her body produces a different kind of serum—the serum of immortality. If he figures out how to get it . . . ," Atem said as his son helped him up.

"Then he can't die—so he just wants the serum from her body," Ryu asked.

"No, Ryu that's not it—he's greedy, think about how much money that could make him? To live forever . . . a "Tuck Everlasting" sort of effect. Think about it. What human wouldn't pay every cent they had to be immortally young, like us? But being immortal we have our own problems—if we get sick, since we can't die we have to suffer until someone finds a cure and that could be hundreds, maybe thousands of years," Tabby said shaking her head.

"How do you get it?" Rick asked.

"Why do you think we all keep interrupting you? The serum comes from her *lips*. Kind of an interesting concept. But see if he does find out then we're all stuck, but it's the least likely place you can think of. The reason we kept stopping you was because if you released the serum then he would find out. I knew from the first time Marshall asked me about Isabelle Jackal that this was going to have to do with Jason and I also knew how crazy he was—crazy to be immortal. That's another reason that I wanted to keep her around our house as much as possible because her parents didn't know, and I wasn't about to tell them that they couldn't kiss their daughter."

"It's falling into place now. Then it was you who put the thought back in her head about the serum that night at The Lotus! And you who sent the dog out—," Rick said and he nodded.

"I couldn't let you release that serum—I'm sorry. Once this is over I'll stop but until then. . . ."

"Does she know?" Lexa asked him as he finally stood up on his own.

"She knows it's there but doesn't know how to release it because if she did that would be a disaster," Atem shook his head.

"But she does," Rick said.

"How?" Atem asked.

"We discovered it a few days ago. You were out of the house and there was this strange bitter taste in my mouth and . . ." Rick's face turned bright red.

"Rick, this is bad . . . this is very bad. Let's hope Jason wasn't there either." Atem shook his head and Rick hung his head, his face burning. He felt his father's hand on his shoulder.

"You look just a little bit embarrassed," Atem smiled at his son.

"Just a little," Rick nodded at his father who laughed.

"Don't worry. I think that if he knew he wouldn't have beaten me to find out, but I'm tougher than I look," Atem smiled and for the first time since he was fourteen years old, Rick hugged his father. Atem was startled at first then hugged him back.

"Well that was a little unexpected," Tabby laughed as the father and son pulled away from each other.

"I don't want my son and me to be like my father and me," Atem said.

"Yeah, they're horrible together," Rick said. "You should see the family reunions." Rick laughed.

"Come on, let's find Kari." Lexa smiled and the group walked into the hallway.

JACKAL'S PAST

While the others were talking, Kari was hanging by her wrists in Jason's office while he sat looking at her.

"Well now, aren't we the little princess? I never thought that the Princess of the Angels would be this beautiful. Now tell me where the serum is," the man growled as she spun in place, slowly spinning on the rope.

"What did you say?" she asked him blankly. She had been watching the fan turn lazily, the opposite way to the way she was going.

"Where is the serum—how do I get it?" he asked and she smiled faintly.

"I don't know. No one does—only Mr. D," she said to the man foggily. "Do you like to play Frogger?" she asked him.

"What is this Frogger?" the man asked her.

"It's a game. Wouldn't using the word play involve a game?" she asked him sleepily. It was hot in the room and when it was hot or when Kari was feeling pressured for any reason, her other side came out. An angelic serenity would come over her and she would become rather childish and disconnected from reality.

"Oh you want to play a game? Well then, how about this—let's play Twenty Questions," Jason said.

"Okay. You're turn," she said, still staring at the fan.

"What's your name?"

"Karina Lacey Richards," Kari replied.

"How old are you?"

"I just turned sixteen a few days ago . . ." she replied, again amusing herself as she spun.

"What are you the angel of?"

"Serenity and Wisdom," she sighed. "Can we play a different game? Can we play hide and seek?" she asked sleepily.

"No."

"Can I ask you a question then?"

"Be my guest." Jason leaned back in his chair, putting his feet on the desk.

"What made you this way? Why are you like this? Can you explain that?" The wiser side of Kari had awakened and she was now going to try and figure out why he was trying to kill people.

"When I was a little boy it was always Damien who got the praise and the attention. He was special—I wasn't good at anything except sports but that wasn't important then. They praised you for being good in school or for marrying the right girl. But not me. I was great in school but Damien was a year ahead of me and he always got his report card earlier so he would bring it and my parents would praise him. My grades weren't perfect—I always got A's and B's but oh, no—Damien got all A's. So I wanted something special of my own. I said I was immortal and they sent me to that place. Then we got out of school and he went to college but I didn't. I married Isabelle and when Damien came back he started living with us. I thought something funny was going on when Isabelle became pregnant so soon after my brother's arrival. I ignored it and when he was born, she named the baby, Derek. A few years passed and my brother was still living with us. When Derek was eleven years old, Isabelle became pregnant again. This time it was with that girl. The moment she was born I knew that she was a freak of nature. She would change into something every once in a while and I began to get curious. I wanted to know what she was, so I began to research her symptoms and they called her a metamorph. As you may well know a metamorph produces a strong serum from their body that can be used for others who weren't metamorphs, to shape shift. But when she was two years old, Isabelle began to take her to what she called a daycare but that wasn't it—that wasn't it at all. She was actually taking her down to see my brother." The man paused to think.

"She and my cousin had been working on

something underneath the old railroad station but I didn't know that. But then one day, a boy I had known from many years before came running into town. I had known him to only have one leg but he had both and that was when I began to get suspicious. So I went down to where the boy had told me and found my brother, my son and my daughter and my cousin. I tried to kill my brother but they had been working on some medicine to heal scars and to close up wounds, so that didn't work. Then I began to devise a plan—a brilliant plan. I was going to take the child and sell her and her serum to the government, but the only things that stood in my way was Tarsal, Isabelle and Damien so I devised another plan. I called my cousin over and then set fire to the house, trapping them inside and Isabelle did exactly what I thought she would do; she gave her child to Damien. Meanwhile I had taken a small amount of the serum to look like Tarsal and acted as if it was me in the fire. Damien was found with Darla and he was persecuted and hung and I got the girl. It was going perfectly until we got on the boat to go to Washington. She wouldn't tell me how to get the serum so I killed her and shoved her in the trunk and then that's where you come in," Jackal laughed maliciously.

"You must be good at something," Kari said. "I mean to devise a plan like that you must be brilliant," she insisted.

"Hey, I guess you're right, but I still want that serum," Jackal growled, once again his mind was on his own gain.

THE MAZE

Rick looked from side to side, they were about to enter a hallway and then he looked down.

"Can't go that way," he said looking into the deep cavern. Suddenly a ghostly face appeared and flew at Rick, making him jump back.

"Help me!" it moaned and then flew back down, disappearing back into the cavern.

"Rick, this is starting to scare me—I mean are we sure we're supposed to go this way?" Tabby asked.

"Tabby, do me a favor. On the other side of this hole or whatever, is the way to Kari—can you jump across it and take this rope with you?" Rick asked the cat.

"I can, but I'm scared."

"That's nothing compared to other things I've seen you jump," Rick assured her and the cat woman took one end of the rope and jumped across.

"Now what, Rick?" she asked him. In reply, he jumped up and grabbed one of the supporting beams of the castle, tying the rope to it. She jumped to a lower one and tied it.

"Have you guys ever seen 'Pirates of the Caribbean'?" Rick asked and they all nodded. "Well we're going to mimic Jack Sparrow—got it?" he asked and they all nodded again.

"Bunch of bobble heads there, Rick," Tabitha laughed.

"We're going to slide on that—over to the other side?" Lexa asked. Rick nodded and in her hands appeared a rope.

"You're first," Rick said and lifted her up. She grasped both ends of the rope in her hands then slid down to Tabby. They went through the same procedure over and over until it was Rick's turn. He cut the rope and swung over.

"What was that?" Atem asked him as he landed on the other side.

"I think it was just because it looked like fun and because I wanted to have my heroic movie moment," he laughed.

"Well that sounds like a movie," Lexa laughed as they continued walking.

"Yeah, so which door do we go in?" Ryu asked. The entire hallway was filled with doors but at the end was a glass door through which light was shining. They looked at each other then ran for it and walked out. As they walked out the door slammed shut and disappeared.

"Okay, this is new," Tabby said. Before them was a maze made of concrete and on the other side was Jason's office.

"Okay, this might be somewhat difficult," Rick said in a slightly high pitched voice.

"Just a little," Atem nodded and Ryu gulped.

"Well, my best friend is over there and I'm going to help her," Lexa said and charged down the steps towards the grass at the bottom and Ryu jumped after her.

"Lexa! No, don't!" Ryu said, and grabbed her forearm and pulled her back before the ground fell in below where she was just standing.

"Thank you," Lexa sighed to him. Atem walked past them and then just walked onto the hole and kept walking followed by Rick and Tabby. Lexa and Ryu exchanged glances then followed.

"Okay, so which way do we go?" Tabby asked looking from one direction to the other.

"Follow your nose," Rick replied and the humanoid sniffed the air.

"This way," she said and led them down to the right. After six more stops they had reached the middle of the maze but the problem was that there were three ways to go.

"Well, which way do we go now?" Rick asked and the others shrugged.

"I'm worn out, let's just rest here for a while. I mean, I doubt he's going to figure it out anytime soon," Atem sighed leaning against one of the stone walls and sinking down to sit. The others did the same, resting their tired feet. But then Tabby did something that they should have thought of before.

"Tabby, what are you—" Atem stopped. The cat woman had just jumped up and had landed on the top of one of the walls and then had sped off in one direction.

"We should have thought of that before," Rick sighed and Ryu nodded.

"I wonder how Kari's doing?" Lexa said, she was still standing, looking over the stone wall to the hill where the man's office sat.

"We won't know until we get through this maze," Ryu replied.

"That still might take a while, this whole maze is huge," Atem sighed.

"Stop being so negative, Dad," Rick leaned his head back against the stone wall, closing his eyes and thinking about Kari. He remembered that night on the boat, everything seemed like it was going to be okay and that everything would turn out all right but instead it hadn't—she was stuck in some man's office and Rick was stranded in the middle of the maze unable to help. His head started to throb because he had unconsciously been banging his head against the stone wall. She was so perfect—there seemed to be nothing wrong with her, but then there were times when she became frazzled. Those times made him laugh because he knew then not even the Areos were perfect. He rubbed his hand on the grass but he didn't feel anything. He opened his eyes. He was still in the maze looking at the grass but he didn't feel that sensation when you rub your hand on grass. The others were looking at him curiously and then they heard a yelp and a thud.

"What's going on here, whoa!" Rick, Atem and Ryu all fell backwards as suddenly the walls weren't hard anymore. Lexa was in the middle of them, her arms held out, her eyes glowing bright gold, her hands were even glowing, on her forehead the sign of her title, the Angel of Visions and reality was glowing, blowing her light brown hair out of its way.

"Hurry, this will only last as long as I let it, go hurry," she said to them and Ryu looked up at her.

"Go," she hissed and Ryu scrambled off, Lexa's body was enfolded in bright gold light and she disappeared when they reached the other side.

"Where'd she go?" Ryu asked nervously he made to walk out and jumped as he felt a hand on his arm.

"My disappearing act is better," Lexa said to him.

Rick's Revenge

Before the others had entered the maze Kari was strong but now she was nothing more than a beaten and bruised body in the corner that was barely breathing and her heart had almost stopped beating. There were cuts and bruises all over her body and she was in excruciating pain. Jason stood over her with a knife held in his hand and this was the scene that Rick and the others walked in on.

"Put the knife down!" Rick said. He hadn't seen Kari yet.

"Make me. I'll put the knife down if you tell me where the serum comes from," Jason snarled.

"I said put the knife down," Rick said calmly. Kari perked up at the sound of Rick's voice.

"And I said 'make me,'" the man replied.

"He said to put the knife down," Atem's deep voice said as he walked up next to his son.

"You—how could you be . . . ?" Jason gasped stumbling backwards.

"Jackal, I am stronger than you think," Atem said, folding his powerful arms across his chest.

"How did you get through that maze—how!?" Jason hissed.

"I have a few tricks up my sleeve," Atem smiled at Lexa who smiled back.

"You and my brother are in on this, aren't you?" Jason said.

"I knew your brother—and you and Damien Jackal were never brothers—you were dead to each other in body and soul because you focused on your own greedy purposes instead of trying to help people," Atem growled and it was then that Rick saw Kari.

"Kari!" he gasped and ran across the room to her, lifting her limp body in his arms. Lexa, Ryu, and Tabby looked in.

"What did you do to her?" Tabby said walking in, her sharp threatening talons clicking on the floor. Her pupils were tiny but before she could to anything, Rick jumped in front of her, his spiky bangs covering his eyes in shadow, tears running down his face and onto his neck. He let out a cry of emotional pain starting out as a deep growl in his throat then lifting up through his clenched teeth, ripping his jaw open into a loud shout, his fists were clenched as if he was being whipped.

"You have killed your wife, you killed your cousin, you killed your brother, you killed your niece, you're killing Kari and now I'm going to kill you," Rick said and slammed his fist into the man's face.

"He's going to mash him to a pulp," Ryu said

a little while later and Atem grabbed his son from behind, pinning his arms behind him.

"Let me go—Let me go!" Rick strained to get out of his father's grip.

"No, Rick, stop! Rick, there's only one way to deal with this," Atem said

and nodded to Lexa who walked over to Kari and pulled off the crystal from around her neck. "Rick stop," Atem growled through his teeth at the struggling boy.

Rick stopped struggling and his father let him go, then out of nowhere, Atem threw the crystal at Jason's body, it went in through his heart and his body disappeared in a puff of smoke. Jason's ghost was the only thing left.

"Just to let you know. The immortality serum comes from her lips," Atem smirked before the ghost was sucked into a black hole. He picked up the crystal as Rick sprinted across the room and again cradled Kari's limp and lifeless body in his arms.

'*As long as my heart beats I will stand by your side.*' He heard her voice in his head and he closed his eyes as the tears came again. His entire body shook as he tried to hold in sobs. She couldn't die, not now . . . she had come too close before.

Contact B.T. Julian
or order more copies of this book at

TATE PUBLISHING, LLC

127 East Trade Center Terrace
Mustang, Oklahoma 73064

(888) 361 - 9473

Tate Publishing, LLC

www.tatepublishing.com

WALTON CROSSING